SHŌKAN

CRIMSON BLOOD

Introduction

In a world where royalty are the protectors of humanity with the ability to summon power from the Sun, the Ocean, and the Seeds of the Earth;
this ability is called Shōkan.

Those who can summon light, energy, fire, and radiation are from the Hikari Tribe; the tribe of the sun. Those who can summon various plants and influence them at will are from the Shido Tribe; the tribe of seeds. Those who can summon sand, water, and salt are from the Umi Tribe; the tribe of the ocean.

Over 400 years ago, humanity's existence was threatened by a horrifying evil; the Hybrids. This is when some of the most noble men and women realized their true Shōkan potential and took their place as protectors.

With shōkan abilities being passed down from father to son, humanity was able to overpower the evil that threatened their existence. Those who were entrusted with shōkan abilities became the eternal protectors of humanity, thus making them royalty.

The monstrous hybrids that once threatened humanity are now few in numbers. Within the last 15 years all hybrids have nearly become extinct and the worse of them called "The Crimson Bloods," have been completely wiped out, at least that's what we thought.

Chapter One

The Rookie

It was the day of my Commissioning Ceremony, and I was finally going to become a protector of the Umi Tribe. The tests were hard, but I managed to pass them all, even without shōkan abilities.

I didn't have any close friends to celebrate with me, but one thing made up for that: the idea of my mother telling me who my real father is. I thought that she might finally be honest with me because part of the ceremony requires that you state both of your parent's names. Stating the wrong name is like committing perjury and nullifies the entire process.

See, my mom married a man named Dan Siratchi. She even raised me to believe that he was my father. He was always great to me, and to be honest, I respect him more than my own mom because he's the one that told me the truth.

I was around 12 years old and Dan and I were outside. He was teaching me about spirit energy and the next thing I knew he told me that he wasn't my real father.

I tried asking him a bunch of questions about who my real father is, but he said that he couldn't give me any details because it wasn't his role to tell me in the first place.

Although he was right, it made me upset, but now I respect him for it. I should have realized on my own, Dan never let me call him daddy; when ever I did he would always smile and say, "Call me Dan!" as if he were doing me a favor. My mom didn't know that I knew the truth about Dan, at least not until the day of my Commissioning Ceremony.

My mom was never honest with me about much: it seemed that she only told me things that were convenient for her or she'd just say whatever she thought would satisfy me. So I don't know why I did it, but I decided to ask her who my real father is. My excuse was that I legally needed to know so that I wouldn't commit perjury while swearing in as an official Umi Tribe protector.

I nervously stood outside my mom's bedroom door. My hands were sweating, and I had to take several deep breaths. After I pulled myself together I knocked on the door. It was only a moment, but it felt like hours went by as I waited for my mom to answer. 'Don't back down. You are a man now.' I thought.

She answered the door smiling. "Look at my big man!" then she paused and gazed at my troubled face.

"What's wrong? You getting nervous about the ceremony?"

I said in my deepest voice, "Mom, I think it's time that you tell me who my real father is." She looked at me like I accused her of stealing from a hobo.

"What are you talking about? You know who your father is." I looked at her with the most serious face that I could muster.

"Mom, it's okay. I know." She continued to look at me as if I accused her of something.

"What do you mean? YOU KNOW?"

"Mom, I've known for years now. Dan told me himself!" Tears began to form in my mother's eyes.

"Dan is the only father you've ever known so don't act like your mother is some kind of whore-monger who doesn't know who your real daddy is."

As usual she took things to the extreme.

"Mom, I never said that or even implied that? Can you please just tell me?"

"Why do you need to know so badly? We raised you up just fine. Dan taught you the skills that got you where you are today! He taught you how to fight, how to use a sword, how to use a bow, and whatever the heck else you needed? So, why are you worrying me with this now?"

I took a deep breath, almost regretting that I asked her in the first place.

"Mom, I asked because during the ceremony I have to verbally state the names of both my parents. If I don't tell them the truth and they find out then I'll be guilty of perjury. So can you please tell me?"

****

At the ceremony, the officiator directed me to recite the oath:
"I, Kazai, son of Herona and Dan Siratchi, vow to protect, defend, and honor the tribe of Umi with my life, my spirit, and my heart."

My mom hadn't told me who my father was so I had no other choice but to state Dan as my father which was technically true. . . mostly.

The officiator handed me a sword and said, "Congratulations, you are now a protector of the Umi Tribe." Then he whispered in my ear "This is a special sword; I trust that you will use it honorably."

I nodded and took the sword. As I walked off, I noticed that he told the next guy the exact same thing.

My step-dad, Dan Siratchi was there. He was one of the personal bodyguards of the Umi Tribe Princess. He is one of the only weapon's specialists to ever earn that position. Normally, positions like that are reserved for shōkans, but he is the exception. I too want to be the exception.

During my first week, I was assigned as a gatekeeper. Our instructions were very clear, if we saw a hybrid, no matter how big or how small, we were to kill it without question. We never saw any hybrids, not even animoids. One of the guys working with me accidentally killed some guy's dog thinking it was an animoid. He was fired.

We were also responsible for making sure that no criminals entered the Tribe. We had a list of exiles, and wanted criminals that we had to keep an eye out for. Being a gatekeeper was a waste of my time and talents.

I think that the Princess realized this fact because a little more than a week after swearing in as a protector, I received my first mission outside of the Umi Tribe.

My team and I were sent to catch a thief who'd been stirring up trouble in Mums Village. The

9

team consisted of me, the talented and resourceful weapon specialist. A guy named Broadie, the shōkan that specialized in cell manipulation. And last, but not least, there was Juicy. I was unaware of her capabilities, but she was a shōkan. So, I assumed she was gifted. I still couldn't figure out why she would allow people to call her Juicy, but it could've been because she was a chubster.

I met Broadie when we were in training to become protectors. I never liked him much, mostly because he was a jerk. As for his skills as a protector, I always respected him for his cell manipulation even though he never mastered the technique. I found it to be highly complicated.

The shōkan summons water and molecules from the ocean and temporarily absorb them into the body to rapidly reproduce cells. With that technique, one could stretch their body and even temporarily grow extra limbs.

Before our mission, I'd never met Juicy. My first impression of her was that she was a little bit annoying and a major flirt. While we were on the shuttle to Mums Village, she tried to flirt with Broadie and me . . . at the same time!

"What up, Kazai? I know you wanna taste

some of this Juice!" She said loudly while puckering her lips at me in the presence of random civilians and Broadie.

I didn't say a word, although I think my facial expression spoke for itself.

"Can I get some of that juice?" Broadie asked.

"Yeah, but you gotta work for it!" Juicy demanded.

Broadie smiled and said, "I'm willing baby! Besides, Kazai can't handle all that juice anyway! Look at him! He still wears his full uniform."

Juicy started laughing, "All rookies do that on their first outside assignment. They can't grasp the concept of only having to wear the Umi Tribe emblem."

Once we got off of the shuttle, we walked to the Town Hall where we would meet the guy who hired us. Looking around, I noticed that Mums Village was nothing like the Umi Tribe.

The Umi Tribe is mostly powered by advanced water systems, but Mums Village was powered by windmills. None of their roads were paved and all of the buildings were made from wood, including the Town Hall. I thought to myself, 'This place is weird.'

On the way to the town hall Broadie started reciting a song from an Umi Tribe musician named Yung Pako. "You're so talented with making me sick, you're rubber and I'm glue but I don't plan to stick, —" Then Juicy joined in. "Around, I'm moving out of town you see."

Then they both sang in unison, "Not really but, you should pretend that I be!"

They both began laughing. Juicy, still laughing, shouted, "I didn't know you listen to Yung Pako!"

"Who doesn't listen to Yung Pako?" Broadie said. I just smiled and shook my head.

Just then a man came running out of the town hall. He ran with his elbows tucked tight to his ribs and his feet moved like he was afraid of touching dirt.

"Hi, I'm so glad that you could come. Here is a picture of our culprit." Then he handed me the picture of the guy. He had long brown hair, green eyes, and pale skin.

"I'm sorry, I didn't introduce myself. I'm the governor here. Please excuse my manners, it's just that this guy has been stealing from everyone's houses and we as a community are just ready to get rid of him."

Juicy snatched the papers from my hand and asked, "Does he have a name?"

"Yes, his name is Findle, Jack Findle."

Juicy squinted her eyes at the picture as if she was looking for something. "Does he have any tattoos, birthmarks, or anything that could help us identify him."

"Why, yes! He does actually. The last person that spotted him noticed that he had a black tattoo of a dragon foot on his neck."

Broadie said, "Don't you mean dragon paw?"
The governor said, "No, I meant foot."
Juicy said, "Maybe he meant dragon hooves."

"Does it really matter?" The governor said even louder.

Then Broadie said, "Of course it matters; I don't want to attack a poor guy with a dragon paw on his neck when I should have been looking for a dragon hoof."

Juicy nodded, "Mistaken identity."

The governor walked off like he was in a hurry and shouted, "Good luck, I have to go handle something…else. I wrote his address on the back. Just go to his house, apprehend him and let me know when you do!"

The governor slammed the door as he entered the town hall building.

As we approached Jack Findle's house I said, "He sure made it easy for us. But I don't get why the local protectors didn't just come and get this guy."

Juicy said, "Listen rookie, a place like this probably doesn't even have a jail, so I know they don't have protectors. Places like this rely solely on shōkan tribes to protect them and even relieve them of insignificant criminals like Jack Findle."

"Yeah Kazai! Get with the program! Dumb rookie." Broadie snarled.

"Okay, well if that's the case, why don't they have any full time protectors here?"

Juicy smiled and said, "My goodness, why are you so stupid."

"I'm not stupid, I'm just ignorant about the situation in this village."

Broadie added, "Stupid. Ig-nant. Same thang. But anyway, they probably don't have enough crime to hire full time protectors or maybe they can't afford it.

Then Juicy added, "Besides, that's how we get extra pay, by helping little rinky-dink towns outside of our territory."

I nodded. All of a sudden my heart skipped a beat: we arrived to Jack Findle's house. I looked at Jack Findle's front door, then the windows and both sides of the house and saw nothing. Then I looked up.

On the roof was a man with his arms crossed.

"I take it that you came for me!" Jack said before squatting down as if he wanted to get a better look at us.

"I smelt you coming from miles away," he said with a huge sadistic smile on his face.

Juicy never took her eyes off of Jack as she said, "Eh rookie, can you see the dragon paw tattoo?"

I looked carefully and then I noticed it. "Yeah, I see it."

"Do you see the blade that he's holding?"

"Yeah, I do now," I replied.

Juicy said, "Good, you're about to find out why they

call me Juicy."

She paused and said, "So Jack, if you smelled us coming, why didn't you run?"

"Because without you here this place is boring! And without you here I wouldn't be able to do this!"

Jack jumped from the roof and spat out six thin ice crystals from his mouth directly at us. As we all dodged his attack, Jack landed on his feet and began to run directly towards Juicy.

She took a deep breath and her cheeks swelled up like a balloon. She shot water from her mouth like a geyser.

The water sent Jack flying straight into a tree.

Juicy shouted, "NOW, BROADIE!"

Broadie shouted, "Shōkan!" and his hands became larger and his arms stretched toward Jack. He grabbed Jack with his oversized hands and pinned him to the tree.

"Ha! You Umi Tribe trash think you can hold me down! I will kill you all!" then Jack blew his breath on Broadie's giant hands.

They instantly froze. Then Jack busted through the ice using the blade in his right hand.

Broadie's hands fell apart into shards of ice and the remainder of his arms transformed into water and splashed to the ground revealing that Broadie's real arms were still in tact.

Juicy was about to hit him with another blast but I stood in front of her and shouted, "Wait!"

Jack ran toward us with intent to kill. I said, "Wait for it." Before Jack could get in arms reach he fell to the ground.

Juicy and Broadie were shocked. They paused a second and looked at one another.

"Broadie! Restrain him!" Juicy shouted.

Broadie pulled out some energy cuffs and put them on Jack Findle, to bind this criminal and compress his spirit energy, preventing him from using his apparent shōkan abilities.

We stood over Jack as he laid face down to the ground, he shouted, "What did you do to me?"

Juicy said, "That's a good question. What did you do Broadie?"

Broadie just shrugged his shoulders.

I decided to speak up. "I hit him with paralyzing needles."

Broadie shouted, "You liar! We were all here. You didn't do anything, but freeze once you saw this guy!"

Juicy said, "Why would he lie about that? You didn't do it, I didn't do it, Jack didn't do it to himself." Jack growled as if he agreed before passing out.

Juicy continued, "I'm impressed rookie, but when did you do it?"

I began to explain: "When I saw Jack jumping from the roof it gave me enough time to get the needles from my pocket. Then I threw the needles as we were dodging those shards of ice. I knew that landing from a roof would leave a sting in Jack's legs, so that's where I aimed so that he wouldn't notice when I hit him."

Juicy shouted "Dang, rookie! You got skills! Pick him up Broadie. We have to go and have a talk with the governor. I have a few words for him." Broadie threw Jack over one shoulder, and we headed back towards the town hall.

Chapter Two
The Princess

As we all stood in the governor's office Juicy pointed her finger in his face and shouted, "What the HECK were you thinking not telling us that Jack is a shōkan? We were unprepared, we could have been killed!"

The governor flinched with every movement of Juicy's hand in his face. I think that he was afraid that Juicy would blast him by accident or something.

Juicy continued, "He almost caught us off guard! If I wasn't here and Kazai wasn't a boss, we could have been killed! Our assignment was to capture a harmless thief, NOT a killer!"

The governor hysterically shook in fear, "I'm s-s-so, so sorry. You have to believe me! I knew both of Jack's parents, and they were not shōkans. This doesn't make sense at all."

Juicy tightened her fists and jumped at the governor like she was about to hit him.

He said, "REALLY! It's true! He never even showed ANY signs of aggression; he'd just steal stuff from us and run. He never attacked anyone! As a matter of fact, he was always a kind kid, up until a few months ago. I never imagined that he would attack you. And I really had no idea that he had shōkan abilities!"

Juicy angrily interrupted, "Well KNOW THIS! You owe the Umi Tribe 3 times the agreed amount!"

The governor bowed his head down and said, "Oh yes! That's fine, I understand. I just don't want any trouble, please." Then we all heard a faint dripping sound. The governor popped up his head with his face red from embarrassment.

We all looked down to see that the governor's pants were wet.

Juicy sighed and said in a calm voice, "Just send all of Jack's records to the Umi Tribe; we'll get to the bottom of this."

"What do you mean? Do you think you know why he has shōkan powers?" The governor asked as he slowly stopped shaking.

"Yeah, I'm thinking that one of his parents may be a former exiled shōkan of the Umi Tribe."

"That makes sense: if his parents were secretly shōkans then he may be one too. Good thinking." The governor said as he forced a disturbing smile.

As we began to leave, Juicy paused and turned to the governor and said, "Don't try to act like you didn't just wet your pants." Then we all walked out of his office.

The governor peeked his head at us through the window as we walked out of his office and said, "Don't judge me! I have issues…bladder issues!"

When we made it back to the Umi Tribe we got off of the shuttle and we walked toward the Protector Station. Jack had already woken up and the paralyzing needles had worn off, so we made him walk. Juicy was in the front, Jack behind her, then Broadie and I behind him.

Juicy turned and looked at us. "Lucky day for you Jack, you get to meet the Umi Tribe Princess, Lady Tuyette. She's the one in charge here."

That's when I noticed a tall woman with three men surrounding her walking toward us. One of the men was my step dad, Dan Siratchi. I didn't recognize the other two guys.

"What up, Miss Lady!" Juicy shouted with both her arms raised in the air. "Is there something going on so big that you have to come out and handle it?" Juicy asked with excitement.

The Princess calmly said, "My dear Juicy, how many times do I have to tell you not to greet me like that."

Juicy said, "You know you love when I do that!"

The Princess smiled and said, "No, I just I love you Juicy. Don't EVER greet me like that in public ever again."

She glared at Juicy as if she could see into her very soul. Juicy immediately bowed and humbly said, "Yes, ma'am."

The princess addressed us all, "Well, I'm here because I wanted to kill two birds with one stone. I received a call from the governor of Mums Village and he told me what happened. I'm very proud of you, Juicy. You handled that with great wisdom and expertise."

Juicy smiled and bowed. "And good job to you too, Broadie Junior and Kazai, son of Dan Siratchi." the Princess smiled and turned to my step-dad, "You must be so proud."

Dan replied, "Indeed, I am, My lady."

"I'm sure you all know and recognize the infamous, Dan Siratchi here. So, allow me to introduce you all to Billy Woo: he was recently honored with the title of shōkan master. This is Dr. Kyro: he is our lead scientist, specializing in genetics. Billy and Dr. Kyro are here to escort Jack to the lab and possibly his prison chambers. Dr. Kyro is going to run a few tests on him to figure out if he's a shōkan or not."

Jack began laughing hysterically. "Shōkan? You think that I am a shōkan? I can tell you right now that I'm not a shōkan!"

Juicy said, "Liar, you spat ice blades at us! How else could you have done that?"

The princess slowly began to approach Jack and looked him in his eyes and said, "No other tribe can summon ice but the Umi Tribe, so that only leaves one other alternative."

Jack began laughing even louder, "HAHA! That's right!"

The princess bent over and grabbed Jack by his shirt and pulled him closer to her face, "Are you telling me that you are a hybrid?"

Jack smiled, "Give the dog a bone!"

We were all in shock. Dan reached for his blades. Juicy took a step back. Billy changed his stance to a fighting position.

The Princess smiled and let go of Jack as she stood tall and said, "In case you didn't know, we have a zero toleration policy for hybrids here in the Umi Tribe. And just in case your simple mind can't comprehend. That means that you are about to die." The princess pointed her index and middle fingers at Jack's face.

Dr. Kyro stepped in between them, "Please don't be hasty, your Excellency. He's obviously lying. Just look at him. I was around back in the hybrid days, and I'm positive that I've never even seen a humanoid hybrid that has zero beast qualities. Look at him! He has no scales, no horns. He barely has muscles. He's a joke! I'm sure that he was just attempting to get under your skin. Please allow me to take him in and run a few tests on him so that we can get to the bottom of this."

The Princess smiled and said, "Maybe you can run an autopsy after I kill him."

The Doctor said, "I'd rather not."

"Very well . . . take him. And be sure to get those results to me ASAP!"

Dr. Kyro bowed and said, "It's my number one priority, your Excellency."

The Princess began to walk away, "Juicy you are coming

with me and Dan. I have another mission for you."

Juicy smiled and skipped behind the Princess, "YES! Does this mean that my punishment is over and I don't have to do lower ranking assignments anymore?"
The princess just smiled and kept walking.

As we handed Jack over to the Doctor and Billy, Jack smiled and whispered, "Hello, Doctor."

Then Billy asked, "Dr. Kyro, do you know this man?"

The doctor laughed, "Ha! As if I would be associated with the likes of someone like him."

Chapter Three

Bizarre Guest

The next day, Corvi, a member of the Shido Tribe--our closest shōkan tribe neighbors--visited the Umi Tribe. As always, the princess made a big deal about it, so most middle and lower ranking assignments were put on hold so that more protectors would be present for their arrival.

All of the protectors were invited to the big feast to celebrate Corvi's arrival. Dan Siratchi, Juicy, Broadie and I were all there dressed in our best Umi Tribe attire.

To my surprise, Corvi was only accompanied by one other person: a young man with long dark hair. Corvi walked into our banquet hall with her head high, chest sticking out, and backside swaying. I couldn't help but think, "Wow, what a woman."

I overheard others talking and they said that she was once a big time botanist before she became the ambassador for the Shido Tribe. Corvi was well known by everyone in the Umi Tribe and was well celebrated.

Although Corvi was well known, no one seemed to recognize the guy that was with her. He wore a Shido Tribe medallion around his neck, he didn't seem to be from the royal family. He had horrible posture and barely looked straight ahead. Instead, he was gawking at our pillars, chandeliers and the stained glass windows.

Before taking their seats Corvi addressed the Princess with their usual greeting, a long awkward hug. Corvi smiled at the princess, "You look radiant as usual."

"I could say the same thing to you, but I won't." Then both the princess and Corvi began laughing.

"Tuyette, this is my nephew and the son of the Shido Chief, Lucius."

The princess firmly shook Lucius's hand and said, "It is a pleasure to meet you."

"Salutations," Lucius said with a smile.

Corvi's face turned serious: "Tuyette, I must let you know. We didn't come all this way just for a casual visit. We have terrible news, and I wanted to talk to you about it face to face."

The princess gasped, "What's happened?"
Corvi whispered something in her ear.

The Princess announced, "Let the banquet commence!"

She, then, touched Lucius's shoulders, "While I am gone, I want you to treat our guest here to anything that he desires."

Lucius looked around at all of the servers and rubbed his hands together while smiling as the princess and Corvi walked around the corner into a private room.

"Corvi, what is this about?" Princess Tuyette asked as she casually sat down on the arm of a couch.

"The rumors are true." Corvi said.

Tuyette's eyes widened, "No!"

"Yes. People from our tribe have been going missing and, on top of that, some of our supplies are being stolen. There have been multiple eyewitnesses and all of their descriptions match. It's undeniable."

The princess stood up, "Are you sure?"

Corvi, with deep passion, said, "I am positive. They are Crimson Bloods."

"Corvi, that's not something to say lightly. Are you sure they can't be regular humanoid hybrids?"

"No, they are definitely Crimson! Because of the previous

thefts we decided to guard our storage units and some of them attacked our guards. The report states that they were intelligent, had horns, impenetrable skin and, most importantly, elemental abilities. There's no mistake, they have the blood of a dragon,... Crimson Bloods."

"This is bad Corvi, I just sent someone to investigate some stolen supplies just yesterday." Tuyette said.

"That means that they could be here too. But don't you find that to be a little odd that . . . well, never mind." Corvi said as she turned away from the princess.

"No! Say it! It's just you and me here." Tuyette demanded.

"Well, it's just that I contacted the Hikari Tribe, and they aren't having these strange thefts like we are. When I tried to get in contact with the Chief, he wouldn't even see me."

"Corvi, what are you trying to say?" The princess asked.

"I just think that it's strange that our territories are being attacked and theirs isn't." Corvi said.

"Corvi, what are you trying to say?" The princess insisted.

"Now, you know me Tuyette. I'm not one to ruffle a bush, but I think that the Hikari Tribe may have something to do with this. Think about it, ever since their new chief came into power a little more than fifteen years ago, they changed their protocol with hybrids. Instead of killing them, they spare the animoids and the non-threatening humanoids. All the while, the rest of us look as if we are trying to wipe out hybrids completely."

"Corvi, did you forget? My father did try to wipe out hybrids completely." Tuyette snarled.

Corvi continued, "My point is that maybe the Hikari Tribe became allies with the Crimsons and now they are using them to gain control over all Tribes."

"I seriously doubt that," the princess said dismissively. "Their chief has always been a loyal ally."

"I'm not saying that it's him specifically. I'm just saying that it could possibly be someone within the Hikari Tribe. Who knows? They may even be sending spies."

"This is not a time to joke, Corvi." The princess insisted.

"You're right, we need to focus on the Crimsons for now. And how to stop them."

The Princess paused for a moment then said, "You know, one of my pupils and her team caught a man who claimed to be a hybrid, but he looked nothing like one: he actually looked human. We think he's just a nut-job who's actually a descendant of an exiled shōkan. I should be getting his blood results in tomorrow morning."

Corvi looked shocked, "Is that even possible? I thought the Umi Tribe has always preferred execution over exile."

"Eh, you're right? I wonder why I didn't think about that. Wow, now I'm really starting to get worried."

"Aw, don't worry, honey: everything's going to work out. I'm sure of that." Corvi embraced Princess Tuyette as she continued, "We'll definitely think of something."

****

Later that night, when I was at home my step-dad knocked on my bedroom door.

"I just got a message from the Princess." He said as soon as I answered. "She wants you at the station before dawn. They said that you were requested for a special assignment."

"Requested?" I was shocked.
"Yeah, by some governor of some village. He was impressed by your skills and wouldn't agree to some assignment unless you could be there."

I smiled, "Wow, that must be the governor of Mums Village! That's pretty cool, being requested and all. You better watch out Dan, I'm coming for your job!"

Dan smiled, "Good job, kid."

Dan closed the door, walked off and then opened it again, "Oh yeah, by the way, your mom sends a goodnight to her Kazy-Bear." Then Dan walked off laughing, "Ha, Kazy-bear!"

I shook my head, closed my bedroom window and went to bed.

****

The next morning, Lucius was the first person I saw upon arrival at the Protector Station. He was standing outside with his ear against a tree.

"Hey, what are you doing?" I said.

He looked at me and smiled, "Salutations, good sir. The tree is speaking to me. He told me that your nickname is Kazy-Bear, is that true?"

I was a little freaked out so I asked, "Have you been spying on me? How did you do that?"

Lucius responded, "I didn't really do anything but listen. It's a gift, I guess. And no, I don't spy on people unless I have a good reason."

"No offense, but you're kind of weird."

Lucius responded, "No offense, but you're kind of normal."

We both laughed, and I went inside where I saw Broadie. I asked, "You're here too. Where's Juicy?"

Broadie said, "Juicy isn't coming. As a matter of fact, they requested for her not to come."

"What? Why?" I asked.

"Well, the governor of Mums Village specifically requested that she'd never come back because she made him piss himself. So I assume that whatever our mission is, that's where it'll be."

At that moment, Lady Tuyette, Corvi, Dan, Billy, Lucius and a few other protectors, whom I didn't recognize, walked in. The princess got everyone's attention by merely clearing her throat.

"Good morning, and thank you all for meeting here this early."

"It's not like we had a choice," Broadie mumbled inaudibly.

"As some of you know there have been rumors that the Crimson Bloods have somehow returned." The princess continued, "I'm here to let you know that this rumor is most likely true, and we will confirm it today."

Everyone became flustered as the princess continued: "Not to worry everyone! We have constructed a plan to not only confirm that we are dealing with Crimson Bloods, but also show them that we mean business! We believed that they were extinct along with the monsteroid hybrids, but now that they've decided to show their ugly heads again, we will make them wish that they were extinct!"

We all cheered creating a powerful war cry. Everyone but Lucius was amped up.

"Okay men! Settle down, settle down," Corvi spoke up. "In my tribe the alleged Crimson Bloods have been stealing from our storage units filled with various foods, clothing and even weapons. So assume that the hybrids that you face will be armed plus have elemental abilities. Here's the plan: now, because we know that the hybrids are targeting storage units we will send one unit to Mums Village. This storage unit is already packed with everything that the Hybrids have been known to steal. But, what the hybrids don't know is that some of you will also be in the storage unit, waiting for them. When they break in, YOU BREAK THEM!"

Everyone cheered in agreement.

"Then, you will bring back at least one of them alive, and we will see what kind of information we can get out of it." Corvi continued.

The princess added, "Kazai, Broadie, Steve, and Lucius of

the Shido Tribe, you are going on this assignment. You four are Team Alpha. Lucius specializes in sensory, so he'll be able to tell you when the Crimsons are coming long before they get there. And because he is not only our guest but also the son of the Shido Tribe Chief, he is not to participate in ANY combat whatsoever. The storage unit will be put on the shuttle in less than an hour, so you'll need to get to the shuttle as soon as you leave here."

Dan looked at me and I think that he could tell by the look on my face that I was a little worried. Dan spoke up, "My Lady, do you think that a four man squad is enough. What if they are outnumbered by the hybrids?"

"I have taken that into consideration. Corvi informed us that her witnesses have never seen more than two hybrids together at a time. Are there any more questions?" The princess asked.

No one spoke.

"If there are no further questions, team Alpha, you are dismissed. Everyone else, we are heading to Dr. Kyro's lab to get the blood results for Jack Findle."

Less than a second later, we all heard a loud boom. Everyone ran outside to find that there had been an explosion at Dr. Kyro's laboratory. We all ran there to find Dr. Kyro bleeding on the floor in the corner of his burnt lab.

"He got away!" Dr. Kyro cried. "Jack Findle escaped! Two hybrids came and set him free and destroyed my lab."

The princess became furious, "TEAM ALPHA! New plan! Lucius, use your sensory skills to find the hybrids. The rest of you, take those hybrids down by any means necessary, and bring Jack back! And if you can, keep this quiet. We don't want to cause a panic."

Just as we were leaving, the princess calmly asked Dr. Kyro, "What were the results? Is Jack a shōkan or a hybrid?"

The doctor said, "I saw no signs of him being a hybrid. And his records indicate that he is not a shōkan. Perhaps he was lying about his identity and he is not the real Jack Findle."

The Princess just stood in a daze for a second and before saying, "We need to get you to the infirmary."

Once out of the laboratory, which was still smoking, we saw that the sun was rising as we followed behind Lucius who was running at an abnormal high-speed. I shouted to him, "Hey Lucius! How do you know this is the way that they went?"

"I don't!" He yelled.

We ran to a wooded area, and Lucius slowly and seductively walked up to an oak tree. He put both hands on the tree like he was holding a woman's waist and whispered, "I'm sorry to bother you so early in the morning, but I need your help. We are looking for some dangerous hybrids. Do you know where they are?" He put his ear up against the tree as if to listen to it talk.

Steve shouted, "Are you freaking serious? You're wasting time! They are getting away!"

Lucius ignored him.

Broadie became frustrated too, "Bro! What the heck are you doing?"

I said, "Just wait he knows what he's doing."

Lucius, standing there with his ear to the tree said, "Oh, that's too bad."

Broadie was shocked, "It spoke? What did it say?"

Lucius responded, "He said that he doesn't know where they are."

Steve said, "Let's head into the woods, that's probably where they went."

Lucius interjected, "Wait! He said that the hybrids didn't leave the Umi Tribe yet. They are headed towards the transit station."

Steve shouted, "I thought you said that the tree didn't know!"

Lucius replied, "He didn't know, I heard it through the grapevine... the one right over there."

We rushed to the transit station.

On the way there, Lucius looked at me and said, "Hey, thanks for not thinking that I'm a nut-job. You're probably the only one in the Umi Tribe that doesn't."

I said, "No problem, plus you were right earlier, so why not trust you."

When we arrived to the Transit Station we only saw some men loading a storage unit onto the end of the shuttle.

"That's the container that we were supposed to be guarding," Broadie said.

At the transit station, there were small trees planted for decoration and Lucius went to a tree then looked at it carefully and said, "Never mind." He continued to another just as seductively as before and whispered, "Where are they hiding?"

Lucius put his ear to the tree and waited. Then he signaled for us to stay quiet by putting his finger to his mouth. He pointed to the top of the storage unit.

Steve shouted, "Are you kidding me? I'm sick of this fool-ishness! Don't you think those guys would have noticed a couple of hybrids on top of the storage unit?"

Lucius looked at Steve and said, "Idiot."

Chapter Four

Electric

A muscular, horned, pale hybrid with long brown hair jumped from the top of the storage unit. Something was familiar about the way that the hybrid landed.

Then it hit me. "That's Jack!" I shouted, "That hybrid is Jack Findle!"

Steve responded, "Are you positive?"

Broadie agreed, "There's no denying it! It's those green eyes and that tattoo on his neck!"

Then he spoke, "I'm not Jack anymore!" Jack took a deep breath and blew out a thick cloud of what appeared to be fog or smoke. Everything that the fog touched began to freeze.

Broadie said, "Not this time! SHŌKAN!" Then Broadie's entire body almost instantly grew over fifteen feet tall. Broadie jumped over the frost cloud and slapped his giant hand on Jack pinning him to the ground. "Gotcha!" Broadie said arrogantly.

The men that loaded the storage unit began to run away.

In that instant, we heard a voice laughing. The next thing we knew, there was another hybrid hovering over Broadie in mid air. The hybrid was a yellowish green color, with short spikes on his head: it had electricity exerting from its entire body.

I shouted, "Broadie look out!" But it was too late. When Broadie looked up, the hybrid struck him sending volts of electricity throughout his body.

The water and molecules that was holding Broadie's giant body together splashed to the ground. Jack, who was pinned down by Broadie, was also shocked unconscious.

The hybrid continued laughing. Steve pulled out his blade and tried to attack the Hybrid, but the hybrid just grabbed Steve's blade with his bare hands and sent an electrical current through the blade electrocuting Steve.

I began to approach with caution, especially after I noticed that neither Broadie, Jack, nor Steve were moving.

Lucius said, "I'd be careful if I were you."

I pulled out my sword, but instead of attacking the hybrid,

I sliced one of the trees a couple of times. Lucius shouted, "What are you doing? That tree didn't hurt anybody! Does his life mean nothing?"

I put my sword back in its sheath, and when the hybrid attacked me I used the small tree as my weapon.

Lucius sat down with his legs folded and began talking to another tree, "I get it now. If he had used his sword, the hybrid would have just electrocuted him. But because electricity does not travel through wood so easily, he's able to fend off the hybrid with that tree. Although that was smart, I don't think it'll be enough. So, what do you think?" Lucius asked, putting his ear to the tree while watching the fight.

It seemed that the longer I fought the hybrid, the faster it became. So I decided to try and take out the hybrid in one quick move, even if it meant that I had to get electrocuted in the process.

In order to do that, I needed the hybrid to chase me, so I ran as if I were afraid for my life. I played my role well; I even screamed. He chased me just as I had anticipated.

Just as he was about to grab me I jumped and kicked off the shuttle as high as I could. While in mid air I turned to face the hybrid while reaching for my sword.

Lucius continued talking to the tree. "I really thought he was going to run away, but now I see what he's doing. He's leading the hybrid to that puddle of water over there where his friend got electrocuted. He better be careful where he lands because he may end up electrocuting his friend again. Well . . . that's if his plan works."

The hybrid jumped in the air to grab me. While in the air I pulled out my blade and swung it at the hybrid. And as I expected, it grabbed my blade and exerted electricity in attempt to shock me, but his electricity couldn't shock me while in mid air. So, I hit him in the face several times with the tree using my other hand.

When we both were about to hit the ground, I braced myself because I knew that both of us were about to be electrocuted.

The hybrid landed in the water first and when he did, I let go of my sword, but that didn't matter because I was about to land in the same puddle of water. As soon as we both hit the water, the Hybrid's electric current hit us.

We both screamed, and were thrown out of the water. To my surprise, I was still conscious. My body began shaking involuntarily, but I managed to pull myself up.

The hybrid looked at me and shouted, "How did you do that? Why aren't you fried like the others?"

Lucius interrupted, "Because in order for you to be fried by electricity there must be resistance for your electrical current and while you guys were in mid air, the electricity didn't have any resistance. I have no idea why he isn't fried after getting caught in it's current once you guys landed. There was plenty of resistance on the ground. To be blunt, Kazai should probably be dead right now. I'm shocked right now... get it, SHOCKED!"

As Lucius giggled, I spoke up, "It-It definitely hurt me... but I honestly didn't think that I would make it out of that."

Lucius responded, "But yet, you did anyway. I assume that you decided to risk your life for the sake of the Umi Tribe. Am I correct?"

I nodded.

"Very commendable, you have my respect," Lucius added.

Until that moment, I didn't even know that I wanted the respect of that weirdo.

"But I don't get it? How could I get electrocuted by my own attack?" The hybrid asked.

"Do you see that wet stuff over there?" Lucius said. "It's called water. It can be used as an electrical current enhancer even for your own electricity."

The hybrid yelled, "But I can normally handle my own fire power even in water! What did you do to me?"

Then I spoke up, "It's the salt water." The hybrid looked confused. Then I stood straight. "I know that in order for shōkans like Broadie to use his technique he has to summon water from the ocean, or salt water in this case. With that being said, I know that salt water can enhance how electricity travels."

The hybrid snarled at me and tried to run toward me but passed out before he could reach me.

Lucius said, "Good job, but aren't you forgetting something."

I remembered what Dr. Kyro said, "Jack Findle escaped. Two hybrids came and set him free."

Before I could even finish processing the thought, a shadow covered my entire body.

Lucius cried, "Look out!" But before I could turn around I was sent flying into a shuttle.

Chapter Five

The Bull

Moments later, I awoke and saw a huge bull-like hybrid. He was about seven feet tall with massive horns and a dragon foot tattooed on his chest. He walked over to Jack and had the other hybrid on his shoulder. I looked around and saw Broadie and Steve just lying there motionless. I continued to look, but I didn't see Lucius anywhere.

"Where's Lucius?" I shouted.

The bull-like hybrid said in a very low deep voice, "I thought you were dead. You should have just stayed there. I would have never known."

I repeated myself growing more and more angry by the sight of my fallen comrades. As he walked toward me I shouted, "WHERE. IS. LUCIUS?"

The hybrid said, "He's gone. And you are about to be gone, too."

Then I imagined Lucius begging for his life and being killed by the horrific bull-like hybrid. So I mustered up all of my strength and I picked up my sword and I ran eagerly toward the hybrid.

The bull-like hybrid threw the electric hybrid from his shoulders to the ground. As I attacked, the hybrid blocked with nothing but his bare arms. My sword had little to no effect on his body but I didn't care. I just kept swinging. I had no other choice.

If I didn't at least try my very best and the hybrid ended up killing people, I would never be able to forgive myself. The only thing that went through my mind was, 'I have to stop this hybrid. Not only for the sake of the Umi tribe but also for Lucius.'

Lucius' words kept replaying in my head, "Very commendable, you have my respect." So, I kept swinging.

Just as I was getting tired, and began to feel like I was getting nowhere, one of my strikes broke through the hybrid's skin, so I began swinging harder and faster until I saw flashes of light coming from my sword.

At first, I thought it was my imagination, but after a few seconds, it was undeniable. At that moment, I remembered what the old man said at the induction ceremony: "This sword is special..."

My sword was glowing and radiating heat. The bull-like hybrid began to back up and then he jumped backward about twenty feet.

I ran toward him while he stood there taking a deep breath and blew a thick, mysterious greenish-brown smoke cloud from his mouth. It came out so fast that in seconds the hybrid was no longer visible, and the smoke was within inches of my body. It almost touched me, but before it could, I was moved out of the way by what appeared to be tree branches.

"Don't breathe it in; I'm pretty sure it's toxic!"

It was Lucius, alive and well! As Lucius pulled me toward him, his arm changed from wood back to normal.

I looked at Lucius and said, "Whoa! Thanks. I'm so relieved that you're okay: the princess would have killed me if I let

you die on my watch!" Lucius glanced at me and then focused on the toxic smoke.

When the mist disappeared, two hybrids were gone and Jack was still lying face down in a puddle of water beside Broadie, who was beginning to wake up.

I looked around and saw Steve limping towards Lucius and me. Then I noticed that civilians were beginning to surround us all. They just stood there whispering to each other, a lot of them gawking and some pointing at me.

Some of the people whispered things like, "Were those hybrids? Was his sword glowing? I've never seen that before. Who is that kid? Where did those monsters go? He can't be from the Umi Tribe, but he's wearing the Umi Tribe emblem."

Lucius slapped me on the shoulder and said, "Good job, kid."

Back at Dr. Kyro's Laboratory, the doctor stood up on his own while holding his side. "I'm okay, Your Excellency. I don't need to go to the infirmary."

"Nonsense, you will come with us immediately." The princess demanded.

"I SAID I'M FINE!" The doctor shouted. "I am capable of treating myself!" Then the doctor saw the troubled expressions of the princess and the others.

The doctor immediately apologized, "Your Excellency: please, forgi-"

"Forget about it! You've gone through a lot. I understand, you're stressed out. If you feel that you can treat yourself, then by all means, you are free to do so. You are a doctor, right?"

The princess walked closer to Dr. Kyro until they were only a breath apart, and she looked him directly in the eyes and pointed her index and middle finger at him and said, "But next time, it'll be in your best interest to remember who you're talking to. Are we clear?"

The doctor bowed quickly as if he wasn't even hurt. "Yes, your excellency. You have my most sincere apologies."

Meanwhile, team Alpha was at the transit station closing our assignment.

"Cuff him now! Before he wakes up!" Steve shouted, so Broadie and I quickly put energy cuffs on Jack Findle.

Lucius faced the civilians with his arms up, "Salutations, Ladies and Gentlemen! What you see here is a dangerous ice-breathing hybrid. So, please, stay back. Seriously, get back! You there, lady with the facial hair, please get back."

"Come on guys! We have to get back to the station!" Steve demanded.

When we arrived, there were many protectors waiting for us. They bombarded us with questions. "How many were there? Did you kill 'em? Is he dead?"

Steve told the crowd of Umi Tribe protectors very calmly: "We must speak with the Princess immediately."

One of the men shouted, "I know where she, I'll escort you there. But before we go I'll have someone call to inform her that you're on the way."

"The princess is in the Umi Tribe Capitol building," the same man confidently asserted.

"I could have guessed that she'd be here you moron! This is her office!" Steve rudely snarled.

The guy who escorted us just walked off with his head down saying, "I just wanted to be included."

We all continued into the building, Broadie and I carrying Jack Findle by the shoulders.

Chapter Six
Jack, A Hybrid?

The princess had us to come into a huge room, much like the banquet hall, that it hardly any furniture. At the end of the long walkway stood the Princess and her entourage.

Near the princess stood Corvi, Dan and Billy and a couple of protectors who I didn't recognize. The princess walked towards us and looked at Jack as we held him up, "Is this one of the hybrids that helped Jack Findle to escape?"

"No, ma'am. This is Jack." I declared.

"Don't toy with me! Your assignment was to get Jack: now, where is he?" the princess shouted impatiently.

Broadie then spoke up, "My lady, we were just as shocked as you are, but this truly is Jack Findle. Look at his hair and look at his eyes. That's the same man that we captured before, but somehow, he's a----"

"A hybrid?" The princess interrupted. She slowly walked toward the unconscious Jack Findle and took a closer look at him. "I must say, he does look like him, but this isn't possible?"

She touched Jack's face to get a thorough look at him.

"AHHH!" Jack wailed as he awoke and attempted to spit ice in the princess' face.

The princess didn't flinch, "That voice . . . you are Jack Findle." The princess began to circle around Jack while Broadie and I held his arms as he struggled to break free. "So, tell me, Jack Findle. How is it possible that you were once a human but are now a hybrid?"

The hybrid looked at the princess, "You really are stupid, aren't you? I'm not speaking to you!"

The princess smiled and walked away, "There are many ways that I can find out what I need."

Standing behind the princess with his arms folded, Dan Siratchi stepped forward and spoke discreetly: "My Lady, perhaps Dr. Kyro can help shed some light on this situation."

"Not only is the doctor injured now, but he said that he didn't see any signs of Jack being a hybrid. So, calling him in would be useless." The princess demanded.

Dan smoothly responded, "Maybe you're right. Or maybe the doctor was disoriented because of the recent attack.

I think we should give him the opportunity to tell us any information he may have neglected to tell us before."

The princess smiled, "Very well. We need to get Dr. Kyro in here to find out what he knows."

Moments later, Dr. Kyro arrived. "How can I be of service to you, Your Excellency?" The doctor asked as he entered the room.

The princess said, "I called you here to ask you something." Dr. Kyro nodded.

"Dr. Kyro, you stated that there was no signs that indicated that Jack was a hybrid. So, please explain this."

The princess pointed at Jack Findle.

The doctor's eyes widened, "I-I-I-"

The princess interrupted, "Now Doctor, help me to understand. You specialize in genetics, so how could you miss this? Did he look like this when he escaped your lab?"

"Yes, I mean-No! Let me explain." The doctor said nervously.

"Please do." The princess insisted.

The doctor looked at the now smiling Jack Findle then

looked at the princess. He took a deep breath, allowing all of his nervousness began to slowly dissolve.

The doctor looked at the princess and smiled, "Your Excellency, that creature can't be the Jack Findle that I examined. It's just not possible."

The princess maliciously smiled back at Dr. Kyro, "We've already examined him, and everyone here is sure that he is the same Jack Findle. But, just to be certain, why don't you get a blood sample from the hybrid, and we'll compare it to the sample that you have of Jack Findle's blood."

Dr. Kyro smirked, "That's simply impossible Your Excellency. All of my progress was destroyed in my laboratory, including Jack Findle's DNA samples."

Then Jack shouted, "Why don't you just tell them doctor? It's not like there anything that they can do about it now!" The Doctor's face changed from pleasant into deep aggression.

"Tell us WHAT?" the princess demanded.

Jack began to laugh hysterically and confidently. He held back his head, "Dr. Kyro is th–"

Before Jack could finish his sentence, Dr. Kyro pulled a dagger from his jacket and quickly threw it in my direction. The dagger pierced Jack Findle in his throat. Jack's body was hit so hard that he flew out of our hands. Two of the protectors that stood near the princess immediately grabbed Jack's bleeding and shaking body and took him out of the room.

"Why did you do that?" The princess shouted, stomping furiously toward the doctor.

"It's like you said, Your Excellency. We are of the Umi Tribe; we have a zero toleration policy for hybrids. Am I not correct?" Dr. Kyro said with malice in his voice.

The princess stood over the doctor, "What are you trying to hide?"

"Please, don't confuse my motives, Your Excellency. The only thing that I was trying to hide is my own shame. I'm ashamed that I missed such a phenomenon. I can't begin to describe to you how sorry I am for my negligence." The doctor said.

The princess continued to stare at the doctor while clenching her fists.

Dr. Kyro passionately continued, "I could have never predicted that his cells would change him from human to hybrid."

Dan spoke up, "Then why kill the Hybrid? What was he going to say that you didn't want us to know?"

"Please, don't confuse my motives," Dr. Kyro repeated calmly. "I didn't kill that thing because of what he was saying. I killed it because—"

Corvi interrupted, "May I, Princess Tuyette."

The princess never took her eyes off of the doctor, "Yes, Corvi, your opinion is highly valued here. Please go ahead."

Corvi stepped forward, "As a scientist myself, I've studied not only plants but also the human body and I must say that a transformation like this is completely unheard of. So, I don't believe that the doctor saw this coming. Besides, there's also something that we haven't considered."

The princess then looked at Corvi as she continued. "We haven't considered that Jack may have transformed after he left Dr. Kyro's laboratory. And if that's the case, then the doctor would not have seen any signs of him being a hybrid."

Corvi, then, turned to Dr. Kyro. "So Doctor, is that what happened? Was Jack in human form when he escaped your lab?"

The doctor closed his eyes and smirked a little. Then he looked directly at the princess and said, "Yes. That's exactly what happened."

"There you have it. The only thing this man is guilty of is being negligent." Corvi said with confidence.

The princess slowly walked to her throne and took a seat. "Listen up! I've made a decision. Dr. Kyro, you are hereby on probation until we understand what's going on with this hybrid situation. That means that you are not to interfere with our investigation concerning Jack Findle. Understood?"

Dr. Kyro bowed, "Wise decision, Your Excellency."

"You are dismissed doctor!" The princess shouted.

The room was in complete silence as the doctor slowly limped out. "Where was that limb when he came in?" Lucius whispered jokingly. I just shook my head.

"Alright, everyone. If there is nothing else, then you are all dis—"

"Please wait, Your Majesty!" Steve interrupted the princess, "We still have one order of business to tend to."

"This guy is not who he says that he is!" Steve said, pointing directly at me.

Chapter Seven
Herona's Secret

I was confused, "What are you talking about?"

"Don't deny it! You're a shōkan! I saw your blade glowing!" Steve shouted.

"My sword did that on it's own. The old man said it was special."

"Old man? What old man?"

"The old man that gave me my blade during the induction ceremony. He said that the blade was special."

"The officiator? That old bag tells everybody that! Your blade was glowing because you made it glow!" Steve shouted.

Lucius then jumped in front of Steve, "Yeah, he made it glow, and it was AWESOME! Kazai was protecting everyone from this ginormous monster hybrid! He was swinging his sword and it barely had any effect at first; but he kept going, even though he was just electrocuted by another hybrid. Anyway, his sword started glowing as if it was generating heat, which scared the hybrid away. Before it left it tried to kill Kazai with some poisonous smoke, but I pulled him out of the way just in time. It was totally AWESOME! Just saying. Just saying."

The princess looked at Steve and calmly said, "Is that accurate? Is that what happened?

Steve looked a little puzzled, "Yes your majesty, that's exactly what happened."

Then Steve looked at me and said, "It seems to me that Kazai is from the Hikari Tribe. I saw that technique once in the Hikari Play Book."

"Yes. Yes. I am well aware of the techniques of the Hikari Tribe, or did you forget that I fought side by side with some of their best men myself." Princess Tuyette said assertively.

At that moment, I felt my legs slowly begin to give out. "Hikari Tribe? I've never even . . ." Then I thought about it: my mother never told me who my real father is. I instantly became nervous, not because I was afraid of what the princess might do to me, but because I knew that I was going to find out who my real father is for sure this time.

The princess looked to Dan, "What do you know about this?"

Dan closed his eyes and paused and then looked at the princess, "My Lady, it's not my place to say anything. Please allow me to call his mother; she can explain everything to you."

The princess closed her eyes and bit her lips after taking a deep breath, "Very well, make the call. Everyone else, you are dismissed. Kazai, stay there and Corvi please come with me."

Another protector escorted Dan to a different room to call my mother while Corvi and the princess went into a private room, I was left in the room alone with a lazy-eyed protector that wouldn't stop staring at me... I think.

****

The princess closed the door behind Corvi and then locked it. She gripped her fist and looked at Corvi then she screamed, "AHHHHHHH-HHHGGG!"

Corvi walked to the princess to embrace her, but Tuyette said, "No! I'm okay. I just needed to get that out of my system . . . it's just that, first we find out that the Crimson Bloods still exist. Then we found of that one of them was once human.

67

I'm not even sure what that means: all I know is that I could have phony citizens out there that are just hiding in the crowds waiting for the opportunity to attack the TRIBE!"

Princess Tuyette paused a few seconds and looked at Corvi, "Now on top of all that we are up against, I find out that one of my own protectors is from the Hikari Tribe. What could this mean? Could he actually be a spy?"

The princess looked at Corvi as if she had an answer.

Corvi was a little shocked, "Well, we can't just assume that."

"What do you mean? Not long ago, you said that the Hikari Tribe may be sending spies!" the princess shouted.

"Yes, MAY-be. Emphasis on MAY."

The princess faced the door, "You know what, I can't do this. I'm calling my father. He'll know what to do with all of this."

"Humph." Corvi muttered.

Tuyette turned around and looked at Corvi and said, "What?"

"Nothing, it's just that I was under the impression that you were in charge here."

Tuyette declared, "I am in charge!"

"Then, why would you allow your father to bail you out? You can't prove that you are a great leader if you call daddy every time things get hard! Come on! You can handle this!" Corvi said with deep sincerity.

"Well, part of being a good leader is knowing when you need help." Tuyette said softly.

"Did you forget that I'm here? We are not just allies. You are my friend. I'm here for you." Corvi said as she hugged Tuyette.

A single tear fell from Tuyette's right eye as she said, "What would you do if you were me in this situation?"

Corvi ended the hug and wiped the tear from Tuyette's face, "Well . . . with Kazai and his family, I wouldn't accuse them of anything just yet. Dan and Kazai have been loyal protectors. As far as the hybrid situation: you're going to have to request another copy of Jack Findle's records from Mum's Village and compare his blood with the hybrid that the Dr. Kyro killed. After all, it may just be a case of mistaken identity."

The princess shook her head, "Mistaken identity."

Seconds later, someone knocked on the door. Tuyette opened the door and the lazy-eyed protector said, "My Lady, Kazai's mother is here. Are you ready to see her?"

****

"Before I see them I need you to bring me all of their family records." The princess said.

I felt like I waited for hours. I couldn't even look at my mother once she got there because I was so angry. I thought to myself, 'Why couldn't she have just been honest with me in the first place? All this time and I've had sun powers! If I had known, I would have been a master by now!'

The princess and Corvi walked back in from the private room. The Princess greeted everyone with a pleasant smile. Dan stood beside my mother, Herona.

Once the princess took her seat, she signaled my mom, "Please enlighten me. To my understanding neither you nor Dan was born from a shōkan bloodline. So how is it possible for your son to have Hikari Tribe capabilities?"

The princess began to skim through the records as my mother with tears in her eyes said, "I didn't want to say this because most people would not understand."

She took a deep breath and continued, "But before Kazai was born, the Sun spirit came to me and told me in a sweet, sweet voice that I would have a son and that he would have Hikari Tribe abilities, and that's when the Sun spirit touched my stomach. You see... Kazai is a very special boy."

I couldn't believe my ears! She was lying AGAIN! This time, to the Umi Tribe Princess!

The princess looked puzzled but before the princess could respond Dan interrupted, "My Lady, what Herona is trying to say is that Kazai's biological father is from the Hikari Tribe. When I met her she was already pregnant, but I agreed to raise him as my own. Herona never told Kazai about this so he is totally innocent in this matter."

The princess paused for a moment as if she was deciding whether she wanted to believe us or not. Then she said, "Thank goodness! This is actually good news. For the first time in history we have a loyal citizen of the Umi Tribe who has sun shōkan abilities."

She then looked at me and said, "Kazai, you are very valuable to me and to the Umi Tribe. I assume that I still have your full loyalty?"

Her creepy tone made me feel as if she had twisted plans for me, but I reluctantly said, "Yes, ma'am."

The princess smiled, "That's wonderful! Good news in the midst of all this chaos! I think that went well."

The princess turned to Corvi. "Don't you think that went well?" Corvi smirked and slowly nodded.

"Okay, everyone: back to your regular duties. You are all dismissed." The Princess said eagerly.

As everyone left, Corvi whispered in the Princess' ear. Then they both walked back into the private room.

****

"I don't trust that, Herona." Corvi insisted.

"Why not? I checked the records, and her story adds up."

"You mean Dan's story. I don't know what in the world she was talking about! See, I know when someone is hiding something, and that woman was hiding something!"

"Even so, Dan is very skilled for a non-shōkan and he's loyal to the bone. You should know this Corvi, we both fought beside him in that war 15 years ago."

"I see your point. But, I have a feeling that Kazai is going to try to go to the Hikari Tribe. And if he does, he may never return to the Umi Tribe." Corvi insisted.

"Why do you say that?" The princess asked with raised eyebrows.

"Because apples don't grow on orange trees."

"What?" The princess seemed confused.

Corvi explained: "The Umi Tribe represents the orange tree. If he's an apple, then he won't have a place to grow here--on an orange tree. At least when he was just a weapon specialist he had others that he could relate to. But, now, he has no one. Although his Hikari abilities may be good for you, considering that you can send him on special assignments designed for his unique abilities, for him it's going to be hell. He's going to long to be with his people, especially now that he knows about them."

The princess stared off into space for a moment. "With the news about the Crimson Bloods, we could really use a sun shōkan in our arsenal." The princess turned to Corvi, "Kazai is our trump card. We MUST ensure that he stays loyal."

****

That night, when I got home I didn't even speak to my mother. I was still angry. So many thoughts passed through my mind: 'What exactly am I capable of? Can I even learn to use my shōkan powers on my own? What is my real father like? Is he even still alive? Does he even know about me?'

I wanted to go ask my mother all of those questions, but I was too angry to even look at her so I knew I couldn't speak to her. I thought that she would come to me and tell me everything, but she never did. Because she never came, every moment that passed made me more and more angry. To ease my mind I tried to make my sword glow and radiate heat like before, but for some reason I couldn't do it.

Chapter Eight

Umi Tribe Hero

The next day, I awoke to breakfast in bed served by my mom, who was smiling. "What's this?" I asked.

"I felt a little guilty about yesterday, so I made you breakfast."

"Are you going tell me everything now?" I asked.

"Please, Kazai, just give me a little more time to get my words together, and I promise I'll tell you soon. Just not right now." She said as she turned her back.

"Typical." I nodded. "I waited 17 years, I guess I could wait 17 more days." I said sarcastically.

I ate my breakfast, which was pretty good, but not good enough to make up for my mother's lies: nonetheless, still pretty good. After breakfast I got dressed for work, and I went on my way.

On the way to work it seemed like the birds were chirping

louder than usual and the sunrise was more colorful than I've ever seen. Citizens greeted me as if I they knew me. One even asked me for my autograph, which was really strange. Protectors have always been admired but never treated like rock stars.

When I walked into Protector Station, the first thing I heard was, "SURPRISE!" All of the Protectors of the Umi Tribe were there, including Princess Tuyette, Corvi and Lucius. I stood there with my mouth wide open in awe.

There was a banner that read: 'Kazai: Umi Tribe Hero'. Everyone sang "For He's a Jolly Good Fellow" in my honor. Then they that sang a song called "Slippy Slide" by Yung Pako. Although the song is terrible, it made me feel sort of special, especially when some of the protectors summoned geysers of water and used them to surf me across the room as they sang the song.

Everyone congratulated me for capturing Jack Findle and protecting everyone from the bull-like hybrid. The celebration didn't last very long. It seemed as if only moments went by before the princess got everyone's attention.

"Thank you for celebrating this wonderful young man with me! He truly is the Umi Tribe Hero!"
Everyone cheered as the princess continued. "Now go back to your regular duties as we continue to show our appreciation to the Umi Tribe's trump card, Kazai!"

Everyone continued to cheer as they all went their separate ways.

As people began to exit the building, Steve came up to me and said, "You see this, Kazai. This would not be possible if I didn't tell the princess about your amazing skills. Don't forget that."

"Right," I said sarcastically.

Then Broadie walked up to me, "What's up, bro! Congrats. You want to hang out later?"

I was confused because he never wanted to hang out with me before, so I said, "No, not really."

"That's cool. Holla at you later, bro!" He said as he walked out of the Station.

Then Juicy walked up to me, "You best not let all this go to your head, Pretty Boy! Everybody else might have to suck up to you, but I'm not going to do it!"

"What do you mean have to?" I asked.

Juicy froze for a second, "Nothing, it's just that Lady Tuyette wants to make sure you feel welcome here."

"Why wouldn't I feel welcome?"

"Because! You're the only one here that's from the Hikari Tribe."

"Well, I never really had anyone I could relate to here, so what's the difference?" I asked sardonically .

Juicy responded, "I don't know!" She leaned in closer to me and said, "And just so you know:this conversation never happened."

As Juicy walked off, the princess, Corvi, Lucius, Dan and another Protector I didn't know walked up to me. The princess greeted me with a firm hug while the others shook my hand. The princess began to say how she was so happy to have me as a protector of the Umi Tribe, but while she was talking I couldn't help but think about what Juicy said.

I thought to myself, 'I really don't have anyone I can relate to. How will I even learn to use my shōkan powers?'

So, as soon as the princess stopped speaking I said, "Princess, I appreciate all of this, but it's truly not necessary. I only did what everyone else here does everyday."

The princess smiled, "We aren't just celebrating your accomplishments; we're celebrating your Hikari Tribe abilities."

"About that: How will I learn more about my abilities? Don't you think I'll need to find someone from the Hikari Tribe to teach me?" I asked.

Corvi and the princess both glared at each other for a second. Then the princess responded, "I'm glad you asked because that's what I was about to tell you. Master Kim Lee here will be training you to gain better control of your abilities."

I looked at the Umi Tribe emblem that he wore on his uniform. I was a totally confused, "Is he from the Hikari Tribe?"

"No, but he's a very high ranking shōkan. If anyone here can teach you, he can."

I began to get a little frustrated. "But how?"

Then the Princess smiled at me as if she was forcing herself to. "Just give it a shot, and tell me what you think tomorrow."

I didn't like the idea: it made no sense to me, but I reluctantly agreed.

At the Umi Tribe Training Grounds, I met with Master Kim Lee.

"Greetings, Kazai. Dan Siratchi has informed me that he has taught you about spirit energy. Is that correct?"

"Yes, sir."

"Great, because that is the center of our lesson for today. So tell me what you know about it so far."

"I know that shōkans focus their spirit energy to one point to summon. Dan also taught me that anyone can use spirit energy. He showed me that by disbursing spirit energy as a non-shōkan you can hit harder, run faster, jump higher, aim more precisely, and increase your overall endurance."

"That's good. So I assume you've mastered how to use spirit energy. Is that correct?"

"Uh, more or less." I said.

"Great, now take out your sword."

I took my sword from its sheath as Master Kim Lee instructed. "Now focus your attention on the sword. Just keep looking at it like this." Master Kim Lee said as he demonstrated what he wanted me to do.

I focused my energy, but nothing happened. "Why isn't anything happening?"

"Probably because you're focusing your energy improperly. Let me ask you a question: Did you make your sword glow since you chased away that hybrid?"

I stabbed my sword into the ground and said, "No, I've

tried, but nothing happened. That's why I need someone that actually knows what they're doing to teach me!"

Then Master Kim Lee smiled and said, "That's why I'm here: to teach you. Now keep trying."

We continued to train for hours to no avail. We tried focusing and reenacting what happened when I fought the hybrid. He even convinced me to try some stupid poses to trigger my power.

This guy did not know what he was doing. The only reason I even put up with him is because the princess told me to. So, I tried it for a day because if it didn't work, I would be able to try something else.

Chapter Nine

Confrontation

The next day, the very first thing that I did was go to meet with the princess. I arrived there an hour early because I wanted to make sure that I was the first person she spoke with. When she arrived to her office, I greeted her before her protectors could even open the door.

"Your majesty, I've trained with Master Kim Lee, and I've had no progress. May we now contact a trainer from the Hikari Tribe?"

"No! You only tried for one day. You think that if you plant a seed that you'll be able to reap the harvest on the next day?"

One of her protectors whispered to the other, "She's been hanging around Corvi for too long. Now she's giving people old Shido Tribe proverbs."

The princess continued, "Master Kim Lee is an excellent trainer. He trained nearly half of the shōkans in my father's territory. So, be grateful."

"Princess, I understand that he is a great Umi Tribe trainer, but in this case I need a trainer from the Hikari Tribe. That's the only—"

"Now you listen! You will train with Master Kim Lee and I will not contact the Hikari Tribe for something as futile as a trainer!"

"But-B—"

"It was nice talking to you, Kazai, but I have real work to do. I expect you to meet with Master Kim Lee today. And, just in case you didn't know, THAT'S AN ORDER!"

So I ended up at the training ground… again.

"What's wrong, Kazai? Why the long face?" Master Kim Lee said while smiling with his arms behind his back.

I didn't say anything. I just sat there on an old stump.

"If you don't want to train today, that's fine. We can just sit here." Then he laughed and muttered to himself, "I get paid either way."

At that moment, I saw an old man in a distance walking with a staff in his hand. It was the old man from the induction ceremony. Master Kim Lee shouted to him, "Hey! I thought you were retired old friend! Shouldn't you be at home napping?"

While Master Kim Lee was distracted, I walked off so that I could train on my own. I figured that there was no need to completely waste my time. So, I tried to remember how I felt when I was fending off the hybrid and tried to remember how I focused all of my energy into every swing of my sword.

I remembered that I was afraid, yet determined to protect the Umi Tribe. I felt like I didn't have a chance to stop the hybrid unless I gave everything I had.

Then, just as I felt I was making a breakthrough, I noticed that Master Kim Lee was gone from where I left him.

"Hello there." Master Kim Lee said as he crept up behind me.

"How did you get over here so fast?" I asked.

"Don't be concerned about that. Why won't you let me train you?"

"Because." I said.

"Because is not an answer! Tell me now!"

I looked at Master Kim Lee straight in the eyes and said, "No offense to you. I respect that you're a highly skilled Umi

Tribe trainer, but I don't need an Umi Tribe trainer. I need a trainer from the Hikari Tribe!"

"You know, you may be right, but the Hikari Tribe is a long way from here. You expect one to just travel all that way just to train one person. We can't ask that. The last time the Umi Tribe asked the Hikari Tribe for anything was when our tribe was coming under attack. And that was over 15 years ago!"

That's when it dawned on me: Why ask them to come to me? I could go to them and come back after my training. On top of that, I may even have a chance to meet my dad. I became so excited that I just dropped my sword and ran off.

"Wait Kazai! Where are you going?" Master Kim Lee shouted.

"I have to talk to the princess about something! I'll see you later!"

As I ran, I thought to myself, 'Surely the princess will let me take a leave to train. I'll come back stronger. I could meet my dad. Everybody wins!' I could just taste the victory as I ran to the Capitol Building, but when I arrived the princess refused to see me.

Her assistant said, "The princess says that your assignment for today is to train with Master Kim Lee, and she is too busy at the moment to speak with you."

Then, I heard laughing coming from the princess' meeting room. I could clearly hear the princess and Corvi just laughing it up. I quickly devised a brilliant plan: I shouted while pointing out of the window, "Whoa, is that a Hybrid?"

The assistant screamed and hysterically looked out of the window. When she did, I slipped past her and walked into the meeting room with a smile on my face.

"Your Majesty! I have excellent news!"

The princess looked furious. "HOW DARE YOU? First, you disrespect Master Kim Lee. Then, you ignore a direct order. Now, you barge in on my meeting! GET OUT! NOW!"

Corvi intervened, "Wait, Princess: hear him out first. Please, it must be of some importance if he was willing to barge in here like this."

"Go ahead boy," Corvi said while smiling.

"Well, it's just that... I was thinking." I spoke cautiously.

"SPIT IT OUT!" The princess shouted.

"I was thinking about what we talked about earlier. You know, me getting a trainer from the Hikari Tribe. Well, I was thinking, maybe, instead of you having to call the Hikari Tribe here, I was thinking that I could go there instead. That way you're not asking them for a favor: I am. I'd come back stronger, and that way everyone's happy."

Corvi looked at the princess with a smug look on her face that just screamed, 'I told you so!'

The princess looked at me and said, "You know, ever since you found out that you're a shōkan, you've been acting real high and mighty. You better remember your place and where your loyalties lie. You swore an oath to serve as a protector of the UMI TRIBE! Now get back to your training with Master Kim Lee as I ordered!"

Later that night, I told Dan what had happened.

"I wish you would have spoken with me before you tried talking to the Princess. Whenever she feels pressure, she tends to over-assert herself. She's still new to being in charge and she doesn't want to appear weak."

"But, is that any reason to deny me an opportunity to become a better shōkan?" I asked.

"No, but the way you approached her was all wrong. Besides I think it's deeper than that."

"What do you mean?"

"Well, I overheard some people talking. They said that they heard the princess and Corvi discussing how they believed that you would betray the Umi Tribe and join the Hikari tribe. That's probably why she doesn't want you to go there or to have anyone come here. She's probably afraid that you'll like them better than us."

"Wow, talk about insecure. Shucks, with the way she's acting, I'm sure I would like them better. But, even if I did, I made an oath to the Umi Tribe, and I plan to stick to it."

"I know that kid, but does the princess know that?"

The next day, I woke up early so that I could buy a map. I was beginning to like waking up early because people were not up to bombard me for my autograph. After purchasing a map, I calculated the distance between the Hikari and Umi Tribes and how long it would take to get there. I already made up in my mind that I would eventually go, and the more I looked at the map, the more I felt like doing something crazy. I was thinking about leaving the Umi Tribe on my own to find my father and someone who could teach me to use my shōkan abilities.

Chapter Ten

Showdown

I walked down to the shuttle station, but before I could look at the schedule I heard a voice close behind me.

"Kazai! Where do you think you're going?"

I turned around and it was Master Kim Lee.

"You should be on your way to the training grounds! Where do you think you are going? You know what, don't answer that! Just come with me, and I'll forget this ever happened."

I looked at the map then at Master Kim Lee and followed him to the training grounds.

That day I decided to actually try his methods, which didn't work. The entire time we trained I was thinking about leaving to go to Zircon City: the capital of the Hikari Tribe. I thought about what the princess may do if she found out that I left, but it didn't matter. I wanted to know who my real father is, and it didn't matter what the penalty was: I had already made up my mind.

I thought to myself: 'I'll leave as soon as my training with Master Kim Lee is over. All I need is a full week, and I'll come back, I'll face the consequences when I return.'"I didn't care that I didn't have a change of clothes, or that I didn't have much money on me: all I knew was that I wanted to know what I was capable of, and no one in the Umi Tribe could show me that.

As soon as my training with Master Kim Lee was over, I began to walk to the gate that leads outside of the town walls. I figured that if I tried to take the shuttle again, someone would try to stop me. So, I decided to walk to the nearest town and hop on the shuttle from there. Before I reached the gate, I heard a voice call out.

"Kazai! Where do you think you're going?" It was Master Kim Lee again.

I turned around and shouted, "Like I said before, I really respect you as a person, but it's impossible for you to train me. I'm going to find someone who can really train me."

The master's posture changed as if he was preparing for something.

"Kazai, I ignored you trying to leave this morning, but I cannot ignore you anymore! It is my duty to make sure you stay in the Umi Tribe!"

I thought about what how he said my duty, so I asked: "What do you mean it's your duty to make sure that I stay? Is that why you're so-called training me? So that you can keep an eye on me and make sure I don't leave?"

Master Kim Lee just stared at me. His silence confirmed my suspicions. So, I walked away, and before I could take a third step forward, I heard "Shōkan!" Immediately, a high wall of water appeared in front of me rushing from the ground like a geyser.

"Turn around and go home NOW, or I will report this to the princess!"

I tried to push through the wall of water, but it was too thick and powerful.

"The only way you leave this tribe is through me." Master Lee said with a dead serious look on his face.

I took a deep breath and said, "Okay then."

I threw three paralyzing needles at him simultaneously and Master Lee caught them all. The wall of water that was behind me dissipated, but, before I knew it, the ground beneath my feet began to break. Instantly, I was completely surrounded by a formidable wall of rushing water. I was trapped.

I tried to push through but as soon as I touched it, large

shards of salt began to attach to my hands. I fell back and the water behind me pushed me forward leaving shards of salt on my shoulder and my sword--not that I could use it with my hand immobilized by salt crystals.

After Master Lee realized that I had been immobilized, he dispelled the walls of water and said: "Do you have anymore fight in you?"

I was pretty ticked with his arrogance, so I quickly ran toward him and tried to drop kick the old man. But, before I could, he transformed his body into water, causing me to go straight through him and landing in the dirt on my side.

Finally he stabbed me with one of my own paralyzing needles and put me on his shoulders and carried me back into town. The next thing I knew, I was unconscious.

Chapter Eleven

Lockdown

I awoke in a jail cell with Dan and my mother on the other side of the bars glaring at me.

"What were you thinking? Trying to leave!" Dan shouted.

I held my head down. "I don't know."

"Now you're considered AWOL, so the princess has ordered for you to be confined!"

"What? Just for trying to find someone who can actually train me! That's not fair!"

"Whether you think it's fair or not doesn't matter. The fact is that you're in confinement and there's nothing we can do about it."

I looked at my mother who had tears in her eyes.

She stepped forward: "This is all my fault." As soon as she opened her mouth tears began to fall from her eyes.

"I'm sorry Kazai, if I'd just been honest with you –"

"Don't cry mom."

"No! I have to! I deserve this pain but you don't! You don't deserve this at all-- I do! I've wanted to tell you who your father is ever since you were born, but my heart wasn't strong enough to do it... because that meant that I had to face my past and actually think about him. That meant that I would have to remember what we once had, and that was too painful to me. It was just TOO painful to even imagine. I should cry because I'm sorry that I wasn't strong enough for you; I'm sorry that I wasn't strong enough to tell you the truth! Please believe me when I say that I love you son!"

Dan looked at my mother for a second and walked out of the room.

My mom held the bars that confined me and crouched down and looked me in the eyes.

She said, "Your father's name is Kazan Hikari."

Tears continued to flow from her eyes.

"You look a lot like him, walk like him, and you have his spirit. I left the Hikari Tribe before he found out that I was even pregnant with you. I'm sure that he still doesn't know about you at all. If he did, I'm positive that he would stop everything just to be with you."

I felt my mother's warmth of sincerity and remorse as tears began to swell up in my own eyes.

I asked, "Then why didn't you tell him?"

My mother looked away, "I didn't feel like I was good enough."

There was a long pause, and before I could open my mouth to respond, a guard entered the room. It was that awkward crossed eyed guy from before.

"Visiting time is over ma'am! Wrap it up!" He said vehemently.

As my mother stood up and walked away she looked at me, smiled and said, "Goodbye, Son. I love you."

I just waved and thought to myself, 'Kazan Hikari, of the Sun Tribe. I can't believe she finally told me. And it only took seeing me behind bars.'

Part of me wondered if she was lying again, but in my heart I knew that it had to be true.

The next morning, I awoke with a magazine in my face. I read the cover: HIKARI TRIBE PLAY BOOK. I immediately wondered where it came from, but before I could ask, I saw Corvi of Shido staring right at me.

"You are a very handsome young man, Kazai of the Hikari Tribe."

"You got that wrong ma'am, I'm Kazai of the Umi Tribe who just happens to have a Hikari Tribe bloodline."

"Then, why are you in jail? It seems to me that you were imprisoned because of your Hikari Tribe abilities."

"No, it was because I tried to leave the city without the princess' permission."

"If I'm not mistaken, and, please tell me if I'm wrong, a week ago the princess would not have cared if you wanted to leave town or not."

I paused because I knew she was right. Almost all protectors come and go as they please, and, as long as they get permission and keep up with their duties to the Tribe, it's never been a big deal.

"So, Kazai, what do you plan to do now."

"What do you mean? There's not much I can do in here."

"Do you plan to learn how to use your shōkan abilities? I heard through the grapevine that you haven't been able to summon any power since you fended off that Crimson

Blood. Is that true?"

I held my head down. "Yes, it's true."

Then, I looked down and saw the magazine.

Corvi leaned closer, "That book right there has all of the highest ranking protectors of the Hikari Tribe listed inside. I have a really good feeling about page forty-four."

I quickly turned through the pages, and there was a man wearing sunglasses holding two glowing blades. Then I began to read his stats and abilities aloud, "Defended against twenty monsteroids, two humanoids and protected over twenty locations by request. Capabilities classified as a heat and radiation. Known for exerting heat from various objects and weapons to make them more effective." I looked up at Corvi in amazement.

"When I saw this guy, I thought of you." She said with a smile on her face.

I looked at the name, and it read Chase Hikari. I was a little disappointed: I was expecting his name to be Kazan.

"So, Kazai, do you think this book will be beneficial?"

"Well, yeah! This book is awesome."
"Don't let anyone know that you have it. You see, Princess Tuyette doesn't even know that I'm down here helping you."

"Why not?"

"Well, we got into a heated debate about you. I told her that she was being too strict with you, and that she should allow you to leave. It's not like you wouldn't be coming back. Right?"

"That's right, yet I'm still in confinement."

"That was my point! We are SO on the same page."

I didn't respond. We both paused for a moment.

Corvi continued, "Think about it. You're here with all of these people that you can't relate to, and to be honest with you…"

Corvi looked behind her as if she wanted to make sure that no one was listening.

Then she began to whisper, "… to be honest, Princess Tuyette really adores you. You are her ace in the whole, her trump card, her secret weapon. As you already know, the Crimson Bloods have come out of hiding and are probably going to attack the Umi Tribe any day now. The Princess wants to use you as her ultimate weapon because some of their attacks like heat, and electricity doesn't affect you in the same way that it affects the other Umi Tribe protectors. On top of that, you would be the last thing that they would expect from the Umi Tribe."

At that moment, I remembered when I was shocked by that hybrid. I remembered that it hurt me, but, for some reason, it didn't completely put me out of commission like it did everyone else.

"So, Kazai, aren't you honored that the princess thinks so highly of you?"

"If she does, she has a funny way of showing it."

"I don't know if you've noticed but the Princess was nice enough not to put energy cuffs on you. So, you would still be able to use your shōkan abilities, that is if you knew how to use them."

"Too bad I don't know how to use them." I said.

"Yeah, but if you could, breaking out wouldn't be a problem for someone from the Hikari Tribe. All you would have to do is use your powers to heat the bars enough for them to bend and then escape. Too bad the princess didn't allow you to have a real Hikari Tribe trainer."

Corvi looked at the Hikari Tribe Play Book she gave me and said, "I went to a lot of trouble to get that for you. I hope you put it to good use."

"What do you mean?"

"I might not look that old to you, but I've been around for a while. By now, I know that if someone can't find someone to teach them what they want to know, they figure it out on their own. All they need are the right resources."

As Corvi walked away switching, I couldn't help but feel as if she'd given me everything I needed to break out of confinement.

When Corvi left I shouted to one of the guards. He came in, and I asked, "How long do I have to stay in here?"

The guard laughed, "You may as well get comfortable, Buddy. The princess said that you'd be here until."

"Until when?" I asked.

"That's just it. She didn't say when. She said UNTIL."

I couldn't believe my ears. How could she do this to me? I was beginning to see why Corvi wanted me to escape, the princess has gone mad. I immediately began reading the magazine in attempt to train myself.

Chapter Twelve

Jack, Alive?

Meanwhile, at the Umi Tribe infirmary, there were several doctors observing Jack Findle's body.

Dr. Kyro walked into the room: "Gentlemen. Gentlemen," He said motioning toward the other doctors. "The princess commands that I view this body one last time before I take my vacation. Do you mind? I need space to work."

The other doctors immediately left the room, and Dr. Kyro closed the door behind them.

Dr. Kyro slowly walked toward Jack's body. "I knew you were still alive."

Jack looked up at Dr. Kyro with fear in his eyes.

"I'm sure that if you could speak, you would be cursing me now, which is why I put a dagger through your vocal cords in the first place! You've been a nuisance from the beginning."

Jack rolled his eyes.

"First, your body rejected my formula, and, to make matters worse, you became more and more belligerent everyday, making it incredibly hard for me to keep my plan a secret. All you had to do was follow my orders, but instead, you wanted to test your new capabilities openly. You couldn't see this at the time, but your lack of transforming put a major dent in my plan. That's why I sent you back to Mums Village, to stay out of the way! But, like a lost dog, you found your way back to me, that's when I found out that you were just a late bloomer." The doctor said as he pinched Jack's cheeks.

"Despite your past failures, I gave you another chance, but you screwed that up, too. If you'd just escaped like I planned, you would have never been captured and the princess would have thought that the real Jack Findle's identity had been stolen. But, NO, you wanted to fight. Now EVERYONE is aware that there are Crimson Bloods, taking away our element of surprise!" Kyro said as he repeatedly poked Jack in the face.

Jack became more and more furious, but there was nothing he could do because he was restrained to a stretcher and bound tight with straps similar to the energy cuffs.

"I know you hate me, but because you are my creation, I'm going to fix you. However, I probably won't restore your ability to speak because your voice is like nails to a chalkboard."

The doctor smiled then walked to the other side of Jack. He noticed a flower with a note attached. It read:

Dear Jack,

I'm sorry you're dead now.

My deepest condolences,
Lucius of Shido.

"What an idiot, that guy."Dr. Kyro threw the letter at Jack and said, "How could you let yourself be taken down by these pathetic shōkans. To think, I went through all of that trouble destroying my own lab just for you to be captured when you could have escaped... The more I gaze at your face, the more I want to just put you out of MY misery."

Jack turned his head away from the doctor as he walked out of the room.

As the doctor exited the hospital building from one direction, Lucius approached from the other. Lucius glared at the doctor and said, "Hmm...just as I thought."

Meanwhile at Kazai's home, Herona and Dan were having a deep discussion. "I don't care what the Princess is going to do! I am not one of her protectors! I can leave anytime I want, and I'm going. I've packed my bags, and made up my mind. He's the only one that can help my baby, and I've delayed this for too long--Seventeen years too long."

Dan replied, "If you must go, I'm not going to stop you, but I want you to know this could be a delicate situation. If you don't play your cards just right, you'll end up creating bad blood between the Hikari Tribe and the Umi Tribe."

Herona smiled and said, "Don't worry, I know Kazan. He'll figure out what to do."

"But, what if he decides to keep Kazai in Hikari? Can you handle that?" Dan asked.

"I can't worry about that now. YOU HEARD WHAT THE PRINCESS SAID! She plans to let my baby just rot in a jail."

"He's not in jail: he's in confinement."

"What's the difference? He's behind bars! I'll be back as soon as I can. Love you."

"I know. Be careful."

That night, as my mother was on a shuttle to the Hikari Tribe, the last person I expected to see visited me. Before he entered the room, I was deeply frustrated. I was dripping in sweat and was finally beginning to focus my energy enough to summon heat to a spoon, but it wasn't enough to say that I'd mastered anything.

"Salutations! Am I interrupting something?" Lucius said as he snuck up behind me.

I was surprised, "Whoa, I'm not doing anything! What could I be doing? Ha, ha, ha…."

Lucius' face was disturbingly serious. He looked me right in the eyes and said, "I don't have much time. Corvi and I are leaving for Shido soon. But, before I go, I have to do this."

Then he took out some keys and opened my jail cell.

"What are you doing?" I whispered.

"I don't have much time to explain, but you have to leave. You're the Umi Tribe's only hope. Corvi tried to tell Princess Tuyette, but she wouldn't listen."

"Tried to tell her what?"

"…That Dr. Kyro is the one who created the Crimson Bloods. He's behind it all!

My face dropped, "What do you mean created?"

Lucius continued, "I'm not sure how, but he created a formula that changes humans to Crimsons. The worse part about it is that I think that he somehow has control over their abilities, too. Think about it, the ones that you fought at the shuttle station had ice powers, electricity, and toxic gas. All are extremely effective when fighting against an ocean shōkan. Based upon the information that I've gathered, Dr. Kyro has been creating his own hybrid army designed specifically to take down the Umi Tribe."

"I knew something wasn't right about that guy, but I would have never thought that he would want to attack the Umi Tribe. He's in a powerful inner circle, which includes the princess! This doesn't make sense."

"I have no idea why he wants to, but I do know that he does."

"How do you know, anyway?"

"A flower told me."

"What?" I paused. Then, I remembered that Lucius has been right every time that he's communicated with trees. But I thought to myself, 'This guy sounds nuts. So, why do I believe him?'
Lucius responded, "It's like this. When we brought Jack Findle back to the Princess, I became really suspicious of the doctor. When I noticed that he didn't act like someone who had just been   injured, and even more so when he threw that dagger in Jack's throat. Then, as we were leaving, I overheard one of the protectors saying that Jack Findle was in the infirmary, and it looked like he may survive."

"JACK'S ALIVE?" I shouted.

"Yep, but that's when I knew for sure that the Doctor could not be trusted. So, I sent flowers to Jack's room, but they weren't ordinary flowers. I created them to act as my personal surveillance system. That's how I found out for sure about the doctor. He blabbed it all himself while talking to Jack."

At the time, I had no idea that Lucius was so talented or that the Shido Tribe had such useful capabilities, I was totally impressed yet a little confused.

"As amazing as that is, that doesn't explain why you're here breaking me out. Speaking of which, how did you get by the guards?"

"Don't worry about them. They are sleeping on the job-- thanks to one of my other creations."

"Seriously, what do you expect me to do? I'm only one guy. Why break me out?"

"Like I said before, I believe that Kyro is manufacturing the Crimsons with powers of his own choice, and those powers are designed specifically to fight against Umi Tribe shōkans. You have Hikari Tribe shōkan abilities, and just 15 years ago a handful of Hikari Tribe shōkans were the difference makers when the gargantuan hybrids attacked the Umi Tribe. I'm setting you free because I believe that you can be the difference maker, just like those handful of Hikari Tribe shōkans 15 years ago."

"That sounds cool and all, but, in case you haven't heard, I still don't know how to use my shōkan abilities."

"I'm aware, but I have good news. On our way here I saw a sign that read: Welcome to Gomorra City, protected by the Hikari Dragon. From what I could gather, the Hikari Dragon is a Hikari Tribe shōkan who's powerful enough to protect an entire city all by himself. I figure that if you go to the city and ask for his help and somehow persuade him to train you, you'll develop the skills needed to protect the Umi Tribe."

"Wow, that's a lot of pressure. Thanks a lot. You sound like just like Lady Corvi?"

"What do you mean?"

"She was down here this morning. She implied that I should break out. She even gave me that Hikari magazine over there to learn more about my shōkan abilities."

"This morning? Why would she? Humph… well anyway, we have to go now. I've already been here longer than planned." Lucius said.

"See, that's another thing, Lucius. What makes you think that I would be willing to help the Umi Tribe after being spied on and imprisoned for absolutely nothing?"

"I haven't known you for that long, but you don't seem like the kind of guy who would desert people in need. Am I right?"

I smiled and shook Lucius' hand as he said, "Seriously, we have to get out of here now before the guards wake up."

****

It was a clear night, and all of the stars were shining brightly as Lucius and I rushed out of the Umi Tribe Jail.

Lucius said, "Remember Gomorra City is northeast from here. Just follow the white trail of roses."

"White roses?"

"Yeah. When I saw the sign, I wanted to find my way back there. It seemed like an interesting place to visit, but, since we couldn't stop at the time, I left a trail of white roses to remind myself how to get there."

"Cool, and thanks again for believing in me."

"No problem, but you have to hurry. Dr. Kyro could be striking at anytime, and it'll take a whole day for you to walk there."

Some guards came rushing out with flashlights, "Hey, who's there?"

I ran. When I looked back, Lucius was gone. It was almost as if he disappeared, but, oddly, there was a tree in the place where he was standing. 'That tree wasn't there before.' I thought to myself.

It was so ironic: as I got closer to the town walls, I could hear Yung Pako's song called "Burning Bridges." Apparently, he was performing at the same time that I was escaping... weird.

Chapter Thriteen

Gomorra City

Thanks to my time as a gatekeeper, I knew all of the gate's blind spots, so I made it out of the Umi Tribe walls without being seen. I remembered that Lucius said that it takes a whole day to walk to Gomorra City, so I decided to run there instead. Lucius' trail of white roses didn't help as much as I thought they would: they seemed to be nearly a mile apart.

I ran until the sun began to rise, which was the last thing I saw before I collapsed from exhaustion.

When I awoke, I was in the middle of a field right outside of Gomorra City. The first thing I saw was an old wrinkled-faced, big nosed, bluish-gray haired woman.

"Are you okay, Boy?" The woman said to me with a concerned look on her face.

"I'm fine; I was just tired. Say, would you happen to know how to get to Gomorra City from here?" I asked.

The old lady stared at me for a moment then pointed behind her where I saw a huge sign that read: Gomorra City, Protected by the Hikari Dragon.

I was a little embarrassed. "Thanks. I guess I'll be on my-"

"WAIT!" The old woman interrupted. "Why would someone like you want to go to a place like that?"

"What do you mean someone like me?"

"You have an untainted destiny; Gomorra City is where people go once they have abandoned their life's purpose."

"Well, there's someone there who could help me."

"Is that so?"
"Yes, ma'am."

"Such good manners. Let me hold your hand, Young Man."

I held my hand out for the old lady as she asked. She held my hand with both of her hands and closed her eyes.

When she opened them, she looked at me and said, "I see royalty in your future, and I see that you will be faced with a intense decision. I also see destruction. Humph, it seems that no matter what decision you make, there will be some form of destruction. I'd be very careful about the choices that I make if I were you. One form of destruction would be greater than the other."

I didn't know how to respond, so I forced myself to smile. "Thanks, I think." I figured that when she was talking about royalty, she was referring to Princess Tuyette. As for destruction, maybe that has something to do with the Crimson Bloods or maybe what the princess will do to me when I return.

Then, the old lady gave me a bag and said, "I know you must be hungry after running all night. Here you go: this will hold you for a while."

I opened the bag and saw honey glazed rolls.

"Wow. Thanks, miss. . .misses. What's your name?"

"My name is Winter. It was nice meeting you, Kazai. Ooh, look at that!"

Winter pointed to something behind me, so I turn around, but there wasn't anything there.

When I turned back around she was gone. I thought out loud, "Weird, how did she know my name?"

When I entered the city, I stopped at a water fountain to get a drink. As I began drinking, I heard a small dog barking. The sound grew closer and closer. I tried to ignore the sound, but, before I knew it, I could feel the small dog jumping on my leg and licking my hand. Without looking, I began to pet it as I continued to drink.

When I finished drinking, I looked down and saw the face of a human on a dog's body with creepy little human fingers, licking me and touching me. I shamefully screamed like a little girl, and I jumped back but quickly regained my manliness by kicking the thing to the other side of the street.

The dog landed and ran off whining. Some of the people looked at me in disgust. That's when I noticed. Some of the people in Gomorra City were walking around with pets, but not just any pets. They had hybrids as pets! All of them were animoids, but they were still hybrids nonetheless.

Needless to say, I was pretty freaked out.

I asked a random stranger, "Do y'all just let these hybrids run around free here?"

They responded, "You're not from here are you?"

I said, "You think?"

The guy just laughed and kept walking. Then, I looked up and noticed a restaurant called, "Frybrids: Home of the Fresh or Fried Hybrids." I nearly puked, but, oddly, my stomach started to growl.

At that moment, I looked to the sky and said, "Thank you,

Winter!"I pulled out the honey rolls she'd given me. A little later after eating my honey rolls, I did some investigating in order to find out where I could locate the Hikari Dragon. Some said that he was a myth created by the rulers of the city to scare away dangerous hybrids and to keep people from committing major crimes. Some said the Hikari Dragon came from the Hikari Tribe to train the city's law enforcers. There weren't that many people that believed that the Hikari Dragon existed, but the ones who did all said that he lives in a mansion on the highest hill in the city, so that's where I headed.

When I made it there, I saw a baggy clothed, intimidating-looking woman with short hair, standing behind the gate with a sword strapped to her back.

As I hopped over the gate I said, "Hello! Is this where I can find the Hikari Dragon?"

"You've got some nerve, Kid-- jumping over my gate. Who do you think you are?"

"I'm sorry; I'm just eager, I guess. I'm here to meet the Hikari Dragon."

"You can't just meet the dragon."

"Why not?"

"Because I'm his manager! I'm in charge of who he sees, and

you didn't make an appointment!"

"Well, I would like to make an appointment now. How soon can I see him?"

"That depends. What do you want with the dragon?"

"Well, I just found out that I'm a sun shōkan, and I need help unlocking my abilities."

"What's your name?"

"Kazai"

"Kazai, huh? The best time you could meet the dragon would be...uh... NEVER!"

"WHAT? Why not?"

"When I saw you coming up the hill, I knew you didn't need anything worth his time! Get lost you hobo."

"Look, if I didn't absolutely need him or if there was any other Hikari Tribe shōkans around here, I would just leave. But, he's the only one I can go to about this. Please make an exception: there are lives at stake here."

"Really? Lives at stake, huh? To top off being rude and coming here unannounced, you're a liar, too."

"No, it's true. See, there are these Crimson Bloods who were made by an evil scientist, and they were designed to take down ocean shōkans. They could ambush the Umi Tribe any day now! But, since I'm a sun shōkan, I'll be able to give them a fighting chance against those hybrids."

"Wow . . . did you just come up with all that right off the top of your head? Because if you did, you should be writing books!"

"I'm not a liar!"

" Prove it! How do you know all of this?"

"I'm an Umi Tribe Protector. Before I found out about my abilities, I was classified as a weapons specialist. Let me hold your sword, and I can show you my skills."

"Ha ha ha! A sun shōkan is an Umi Tribe protector? Yeah, right? And you want me to give you my blade so that you could use it against me. Yeah right?"

The woman scratched her head and looked up and said, "But, there is something that could be done."

I cringed as I anticipated what twisted thoughts could be going through her mind.

Then she continued, "I was once a protector myself. So, if you could handle an attack from me, then that'll prove that you're not just some fan trying to meet the dragon for an autograph."

Before I could respond, she charged toward me.

I prepared myself as she came in for a punch but followed through with a kick instead. I was barely able to dodge her attack. I really didn't want to fight her, so I tried to talk her out of it as she continued her assault.

"My mother always told me not to hit a lady! So, don't make me disappoint her!" I shouted.

"You'll have to disappoint her if you want to see the dragon!" She shouted as she continued to attack.

I dodged and blocked everything she came at me with. I could tell she was beginning to get frustrated, so I cracked a smile. "I told you! I'm an Umi Tribe Protector! Just give it up."

She jumped back for a moment and said, "Don't think that just because I'm a woman that you could just take me lightly. I was taking it easy on you! But, now, it's time to get serious."

Then, the crazy nut-job of a woman pulled out shuriken blades and began throwing them at me. Forgetting that I was unarmed, I reached for my sword. One of the blades grazed my skin, but I managed to dodge the others.

The lady came rushing towards me with her sword. She swung her sword as if she was trying to kill me. I thought to myself, 'Is she really trying to kill me or just test my abilities?' That's when I ran backwards to create distance between us, "What are you doing! How is this testing my abilities?" I shouted.

"If you can get past this kind of attack, it'll prove that you aren't lying!"

"Well, I'm still here. I think I proved my point!"

"No, that's not enough! You need to fight me like you would fight a man! Or better yet, like a Crimson!"

"I told you, Lady! I'm a bit old-fashioned; I try not to hit women! Just let me pass!"

Suddenly, she threw another shuriken directly at my face. I bent backwards just in time. Then she ran towards me swinging her sword. I began to run backward in order to keep my distance from her. When she realized that she couldn't hit me swinging her sword, she threw it at me. The sword stabbed into a tree that was behind me.

The woman stopped.

I pulled the sword out of the tree, and I swung it in a fit of rage saying, "If I ever start hitting women, I promise, you'll be the first to know!"

When I swung the sword several rays of light blasted from the sword like a laser.

The light hit the woman's clothes and ripped the top half of her wardrobe off. I thought to myself, 'Oh my God! How in the world did I do that? And how is it that the light extended from my sword this time. If I don't get a handle on this I could really hurt someone.'

"You pervert!" She shouted as she held up what remained of her clothing.

I looked at her, "You see, this is why I need to see the Hikari Dragon--so that I can learn to get a handle on these abilities of mine. So, do you believe me now?"

She glared at me for a second, but, before she could respond, we heard a voice shout, "Porsha! What are you doing?"

Behind the woman stood an extremely muscular man with a mask over his face. He had lifeless eyes and long, locked hair. His presence alone was intimidating, not to mention his voice. I was in awe. It was as if he just appeared out of nowhere.

Chapter Fourteen

The Dragon

"Master Dragon, this guy wanted to see you. I tried to stop him but he fights dirty!"

"Well, why does he want to see me?" The Hikari Dragon said in a low rough tone.

"He claims that he's a Hikari shōkan from the Umi Tribe!"

The Hikari Dragon turned to me. I couldn't move or speak. His lifeless eyes glared at me, and it felt like he was staring through my very soul. I was hoping that he would just continue talking to Porsha as if I wasn't there, but he didn't.

"What is your name?"

"My, my name is Kazai." I gulped.

He paused for a second.

"Why are you here, Kazai?"

"Well, I just found out about my sun shōkan abilities, and I never met anyone from the Hikari tribe. So, I –"

"You need a trainer?" The dragon interrupted.

"Yes, sir."

"Porsha, do we have any assignments scheduled?"

Porsha looked offended, "Master Dragon! You're not thinking of wasting your time with this dork are you?"

"I'll take that as a no." The dragon said as he turned around and walked toward the mansion.

He raised his arm to signal me and said, "Follow me."

We went to the courtyard of his mansion.

"What are you having problems with?" The dragon asked me in a low intimidating voice.

"Well, I have no idea what I'm doing. One day, I was fighting hybrids, and my sword started glowing. But, after that, whenever I tried to activate my shōkan it never worked. Well, except for a few minutes ago against Porsha, but I don't even know how that happened."

Then, I looked at Porsha who was standing in the shade under a tree nursing her wounds. I walked over, "I really didn't mean to burn you. I'm sorry about that."

She just glared at me.

The dragon spoke up, "Get over here!" I walked over to him and he said, "Stay still." Then he glared at me with those lifeless eyes of his, "In order for you to understand how to use your power you have to know where it comes from."

"I know where it comes from. The sun, right?"

"Wrong! Our power comes from the spirit of the Sun, not the sun itself."

"Wow."

"There are four main elements of the sun: heat, light, radiation and fire. Most Hikari Tribe shōkans specialize in one or more of these elements. You definitely have the elements of heat and light. When-"

"Wait! How do you know that those are my elements? My element could just as well be fire."

The dragon sat down on the ground and pointed at his eyes, "I have heat vision. I can see more than you could ever imagine with these eyes."

"I take it that you only see in heat vision." I said.

He looked away for a second and said, "Now that I'm blind, I have better insight, which to me is more valuable than outsight."

"That's pretty deep, I guess." I said while tilting my head in confusion.

"Enough about me, don't you want to learn?" the Dragon shouted.

"Yes, yes, I'm sorry! Please continue."

"In order for you to use your abilities you must first understand how to use your spirit energy in sync with the spirit of the sun."

"When I was a weapons specialist, I pretty much mastered focusing my spirit energy, but how do I get in sync with the sun spirit?"

"You have a connection. That much is clear. It may be that you need to simply acknowledge your connection while focusing your spirit energy. Let me show you."

The Hikari Dragon stood up, "Porsha, give me your sword." Porsha threw her sword to him, and he caught it by the handle. That was pretty impressive, considering that he's blind.

"What helps some people is saying the word shōkan. Saying shōkan is like declaring the spirit's power as your own. In other words, it's like declaring that you are connected to the spirit's power. Now, step back."

As I stepped backward, the dragon pointed the sword upward and said, "First, imagine what you want to happen. Then, expect it to happen while focusing your spirit energy. When you feel the sensation of the sun spirit's power, acknowledge it by saying SHŌKAN!"

At that moment his sword not only began to glow, it immediately caught fire. I could feel the heat from the sword even from a distance. Then, the dragon stabbed the sword into the ground, and everything around it was instantly disintegrated.

"A sword like this isn't really built for Hikari style techniques, but it'll do. Now, you try."

I grabbed the still-hot sword and took a deep breath while holding the sword up. I focused my spirit energy and imagined what I wanted to happen. I waited for the sensation of the sun spirit but I didn't really know what I should be feeling so I just said, "Shōkan!" The sword began to glow, but it almost immediately dissipated.

I couldn't believe it, "Well, that was progress. I was never able to do that before now."

"You should have been able to manage it much longer than that! Come here."

Then the dragon grabbed my forehead and glared at me up and down. "You are carrying a heavy burden. It seems like resentment or maybe un-forgiveness. Whatever it is, it's blocking you."

"What do you mean blocking me."

"Your issues are keeping you from reaching your full potential as a shōkan. In order for you to move forward, you'll have to let go of the resentment that you're holding on to. It's literally blocking you from your connection with the sun spirit, limiting your true source of power. So, what it is kid? What's holding you back?"

I thought about how the princess had placed me in jail and tried to manipulate me by making me famous and how she used Master Kim Lee to spy on me and keep me from leaving town. I looked at the situation and thought to myself, 'Well, she was just doing what she thought was best as a ruler. Besides, I knew before I tried to leave that there would be some extreme consequences, so I forgive her.'

Then, I picked up the sword and tried it again, "Shōkan!" The same thing happened. There was a burst of light, but it didn't last.

The dragon began to walk off, "Let me know when you work out your issues."

"WAIT! I'm not sure I have any unforgiveness or resentment. I've already forgiven the only person who's wronged me. What should I do if I don't have unforgiveness in me and it still doesn't work?"

"That's not a possibility! You definitely have something. Think about it, most resentment that causes blockage has become so common in your life, you don't even recognize it for what it is."

Becoming frustrated, I asked, "How do you know all of this?"

The dragon looked at me and said, "Because I was once blocked. And it was because of my own unforgiveness, resentment and malice towards one person... that same person is the one that took my sight and exiled me from the Hikari Tribe. Later on, I managed to forgive him, and, not long after that, I developed heat vision. I probably could have developed that power years sooner if I hadn't been so stubborn. So think back: who do you feel has wronged you the most?"

I immediately began thinking of my mother: 'Could it be her? It couldn't be her. She's my mother. Well, she kept me from knowing who my father is. And I have noticed that I don't bother asking her anything anymore because I don't believe that she'll be honest with me. Could it be that I respect her, but I don't have much respect for her? I honor her but I don't see her as honorable. Yes, it's definitely her.

I haven't forgiven my mother for all that she's done…and what she didn't do.'

I continued to think to myself: 'I can't, I can't! How could I forgive her? The only reason I'm in this situation is because of her. If she had been honest with me from the beginning, I would already know how to control my powers. But, because of her dishonesty, I am now seventeen years behind; on top of that, I never met my father because of her!'

The Hikari Dragon stepped closer to me and shouted, "Listen! You don't forgive someone because they deserve it. You forgive them because you don't deserve the weight that comes with unforgiveness!"

Then, I thought to myself: 'Come on, you can do this. She is my mother; you only get one mother in a lifetime! Yes, she's made some mistakes but who hasn't? I love her and she loves me. I have to remember that she loves me. Regardless of what she's done or didn't do, she's STILL my mother, and I love her.'"

Then, the dragon said, "Look, I don't care enough to know who you have resentment toward, but I'm sure it's someone close to you. So, how would you feel if they died right now without your forgiveness?"

I imagined my mother lying in a casket. My heart sank, and a tear fell from my eyes.
 I thought to myself: 'The next time I see you mother, I will

tell you that I forgive you. Because regardless of what you've done, you're still the only mother I will ever have.'

"That's it! I can see it lifting." The dragon shouted.

At this point, tears began rushing from my eyes. It felt as if weight or pressure was lifting off of me, and I felt lighter.

"Try it now!" The dragon shouted.

I held up the sword, and I shouted, "SHŌKAN!" The sword slowly began to glow and radiate heat. It wasn't as destructive and powerful as when the Hikari Dragon did it, nor did it catch fire, but it was still powerful nonetheless. I couldn't help but smile as tears fell from my eyes. I couldn't believe that I actually did it.

Porsha walked over to the Dragon, "Master, I don't get what just happened. I thought he was supposed to forgive someone. He didn't call anyone or anything, but he was still able to do it."

The dragon turned to her, "You don't have to physically talk to the person in order for you to forgive them in your heart."

"So you're saying that he just knew to forgive them in his heart? I would have just called them and said that I was sorry. I guess that guy is not as dumb as he looks."

"He is of the Hikari Tribe." The dragon said.

I jumped up and down: "YES! I did it! I did it!" I shouted.

The dragon walked closer to me. Even though he was wearing a mask, I could tell that he was smiling.

"Kid, now that you know how to do that, I'll show you how to release it the same way you did to Porsha. But this time it'll be more powerful. How 'bout that?"

"OH, HECKS YEAH! Let's do this!" I shouted.

Chapter Fifteen
Chief Kazan

Meanwhile, Herona made it to the Hikari Tribe in search of my father, Kazan. As she entered the heart of Zircon City, she couldn't help but be overwhelmed by emotion.

She thought, 'I can't believe it's been eighteen years since I've been here. It looks exactly the same.'

Then, Herona heard a voice from the distance cry out, "Herona! Herona! Is that you?"

It was Herona's childhood friend Jackie. Herona's eyes lit up, and they both began screaming and jumping like two teenage girls.

"Herona! Where have you been? I missed you so MUCH!"

"Girl, I've been living in the Umi Tribe."

"WHAT? That's why I haven't seen you. You were practically on the other side of the world! Oh my goodness, I have so many questions for you! Okay, Okay, are your married?"

"Yes I'm married, and I want to answer all of your questions. But, I'm only here to find someone, and I don't have a lot of time."

"Who you looking for? Maybe I could help?"

"I'm looking for Kazan."

Jackie paused. Then she cracked a smile and began laughing.

"Are you serious?"

Herona was puzzled, "Yeah, what's so funny?"

"You mean Kazan Hikari of the Hikari Tribe? The one that you used to have a huge crush on?"

"Yes!"

"You mean the same Kazan who started the Hikari Playbook?"

"Yes!"

"You mean the same Kazan who won all of those Accolades?"

"YES! YES! YES! What's so funny?"

"Kazan is no longer Kazan."

"What do you mean?"

"The Kazan you know is gone. He is now referred to as Chief of the Hikari Tribe."

"What?"

"How could you NOT know this?"

"I... I don't know."

Herona began to think about how every time she heard anything relating to the Hikari Tribe that she would immediately shut it out. She turned off radios, threw away magazines and ignored people whenever she heard that it had anything to do with the Hikari Tribe. She did it all because she didn't want to be reminded of the pain that she felt from leaving.

Jackie smiled and said, "My goodness, why do you want to see the chief?"

"Because he's my son's father."

Jackie paused and said with a determined look on her face, "Are you serious?"

"Yep."

At that very moment, a large crowd of people began running into the streets, cheering and screaming.

"What's going on?" Herona shouted to Jackie.

"It's the chief! He comes into town sometimes! Whenever he does, everyone goes crazy and tries to meet him. Oh… my goodness! Herona! You have to go meet him now! It's your best chance! Let's go!"

They both went running into the crowd pushing through people. When they got through the masses, the first thing Herona saw was a large solar powered vehicle without a roof driving very slowly through the crowd of people. Riding in the back was Chief Kazan, smiling and waving while repeatedly being punched in the back of the head by a little old lady who was shouting, "You old-fashioned, punk! When are you going to give me grandchildren?" Despite the old lady hitting him, he continued to smile, wave and shake people's hands.

Herona and Jackie both shouted, "Kazan! Chief Kazan! Hey, look this way!" But, the chief didn't notice them because of all of the commotion from the crowd of people. At that moment, everything began to move in slow motion for Herona. She thought about her past with Kazan and all of the good times they'd shared. She thought of the many long walks that they used to take and the late nights they used to spend staring at the stars, just talking. Then, she remembered Kazan's nickname that she gave him.

Herona pushed through the moving crowd and got as close as she could and shouted, "KAZY-BEAR!"

Kazan paused.
He turned around and locked eyes with Herona.

"Stop!" Kazan shouted to the driver.

The driver stopped abruptly, and the old lady fell from the back seat into the front. Tears began to well up in Herona's eyes. Kazan reached his hand out so that he could help her into the vehicle. Before they could lock hands, Kazan leaned forward a little too much and fell.

The Hikari Tribe citizens rushed to Kazan's aide, but he quickly hopped up and began laughing hysterically, "I'm okay! It's not like I just sprained my ankle or anything… ouch."

Kazan limped back on the vehicle and he reached out his hand, "Now let's try this again."

He pulled Herona up into the vehicle.

Jackie shouted, "You go girl!"

The old lady, now sitting in the front, said, "Grandchildren, here we come!"

Later at Kazan's office.

"So, now that we're alone. What brings you here after all this time? Wait! That came out wrong. What I meant is that I waited for you to come back for over 10 years, and now that I'm finally over you, you pop up out of the blue. Okay, wait! That's not how…I meant for that to sound." He continued to stutter. "Okay, here we go…I'm happy to see you. What brings you here?"

"I'm married." Herona blurted.

"What? I didn't eve-"
"I know you didn't ask, but before you get any thoughts, I wanted you to know, especially since your grandma was talking about making her grand babies."

"Well, that figures." Kazan said.

"What do you mean by that?"

"Just look at you! Why would someone like you be single?"

"Someone like me?" Asked Herona.

"You know what I mean! You've been gone for almost twenty years, and you look even better than the last time that I saw you."

"Thanks, that's sweet of you to say."

"Well, I wasn't trying to be sweet. I was just being honest, Ma'am. I'm not one for coming on to married women." Kazan said with a serious look on his face.

"I know, I know." Herona said while giggling. Then, she continued, "I'm here because our son needs your help."

"What did you say?" Kazan said with a concerned look on his face.

Herona took a deep breath, "I said, our son needs your help. We have a son together, and his name is Kazai. I'm sorry I never told you. It's just that our last conversation made it clear that you didn't want to be with me, and I didn't want to use our baby to force you into something that you didn't want to be a part of."

"WHAT THE HECK ARE YOU TALKING ABOUT? I LOVED YOU TO DEATH! Our last conversation should have told you that! I was declaring my love for you!" Kazan exclaimed.

"No, you weren't! You said that you weren't going to be able to see me anymore!"

"Yeah, TEMPORARILY! Because I was elected as a candidate for Chief! I searched for you for years! I had to go through therapy! And it was all because of a misunderstanding? Why didn't you tell me that you were leaving, or, better yet, why you were leaving?"

"I don't know, I don't know! Wait, I did! I left a letter!"

"I never saw a letter! Jackie said that you just packed up and left."

"I didn't leave it with Jackie! I left it with your cousin! I forgot his name, but you used to call him the dragon!"

Kazan paused, "You mean, the Hikari Dragon. He was banished from the tribe not long after you left. We weren't exactly getting along back then. He probably destroyed the letter the moment you gave it to him."

There was a long silence.

Then Kazan's eyes widened, "I HAVE A SON! AND HE NEEDS MY HELP! WHAT HAPPENED?"

"It's all my fault. I never told Kazai who his real father is or that he has a Hikari Tribe bloodline. I thought that maybe if he didn't know, the shōkan trait may skip over him but it didn't. To make a long story short: Kazai recently became an Umi Tribe protector as a weapons specialist, but not long after, he discovered that he has shōkan abilities. Out of fear of losing him, Princess Tuyette wouldn't let him leave the town--not even to find a Hikari Tribe trainer to teach him. So, Kazai tried to leave anyway, and the princess had him put in confinement, and she doesn't plan to let him out anytime soon. I think that she wants to hold him there until the Crimson Bloods attack!"

"Let's go!"

"You mean now?"

"Yeah. Let's go now! I know exactly how to handle Princess Tootty." Kazan said with confidence.

"Okay, let's go then. Can you still do that light speed thing?" Herona asked cheerfully.

"Yeah, but that may not be a good idea, saying that I actually sprained my ankle. We'll just take the next shuttle. Besides, that'll give us time to catch up. I want to know more about those Crimson Bloods you mentioned."

Chapter Sixteen
Crimsons Revealed

Meanwhile in Gomorra City, I woke up early so I could prepare to go back to the Umi Tribe, but before I could, the Dragon stopped me and said, "Have some breakfast."

I walked into his enormous kitchen. Porsha was already in there eating like she'd never had a decent meal in her life. They had an entire breakfast buffet.

"Porsha likes to cook and she's not half bad." The dragon said as he leaned against the doorway with his arms crossed. I fixed me a plate, sat down and looked at the dragon just standing there.

"Aren't you going to eat something?" I asked as if I was offering my own food.

He said, "I ate already."

Porsha pointed at me with a mouth full of food and said, "You think you're slick don't you!"

"What do you mean?"

"You're trying to get Master Dragon to take off his mask! Aren't you?"

"Not really, I was just..."

Then I thought about it, 'Why does he wear that mask? What is he hiding? You know what, I'm going to ask.' But before I could open my mouth, I noticed a box that read; "Frybrids: Home of the Fresh and Fried hybrids."

I looked at my plate and nearly puked. I immediately began to set all of the meat aside.

When I finished eating, I pushed my plate forward. Porsha shouted, "You're not going to eat any of that meat?"

I didn't want to offend them and I didn't know what to say, so I froze. Porsha got louder, "What's wrong with you? If you don't eat meat, why would you put it on your plate?"

The Dragon interjected, "Because he doesn't eat hybrid! Think about it: he was born in the Umi Tribe. Isn't that right, Kazai?"

I smiled while scratching my head, "Yeah, I'm sorry. I didn't realize what it was until it was already on my plate."

"Don't worry about it. We're not hurting for food. Right,

Porsha?" The dragon said.

Porsha rolled her eyes and asked, "So, what you guys usually eat in the Umi Tribe?"

I responded, "Well, we eat mostly seafood since we're on the coast."

Porsha said, "Like what? Name something!"

I hesitated, "Well, fish of course. Sea urchins, Kelp, Sushi, Algae and stuff like that."

Porsha just looked at me, rolled her eyes, and walked out of the room without responding.

The dragon looked towards me, "Are you leaving now?"

I nodded.

The dragon raised his voice, "I said are you leaving now?"

Then I remembered that he was blind and didn't actually see me nodding my head, so I said, "Yes! Yes! I'm sorry."

"So, you're going to leave when you only learned that novice technique?" The dragon said as he glared his lifeless eyes at me.

"Well, I have to be getting back. What if the Umi Tribe is

attacked? I want to be there to help." I demanded.

"With the technique you mastered, you won't be much help."

"I think I can hold my own with it?" I said confidently.

"Okay, Genius. But, what if you lose your sword?"

I paused for a second. I thought, 'Why didn't I think about that?'

The dragon continued, "Let's go outside. I want to show you something."

Meanwhile in the Umi Tribe:
Dr. Kyro was standing outside of the princess' office as she approached along with Dan and Billy Woo.

Dr. Kyro smiled and said, "Your majesty, now that our guests have gone back to the Shido Tribe, I would like to discuss something of importance with you."

As they walked into her office, the princess snarled, "Is this about your suspension? Because if it is, you can save your breath."

Dr. Kyro smiled, "Quite the contrary, Your Majesty. It's about someone else's permanent suspension."

Dr. Kyro, Dan Siratchi and Billy Woo stood while the princess sat high in her chair.

The doctor smiled, "Your Excellency, it is my understanding that your prized possession has escaped his trophy room."

"I assume that you're talking about Kazai? Why do you ask? Do you have any information about how he escaped?" The princess said while glaring at the doctor.

"Quite the contrary, Your Majesty. I just wanted to be sure that your were okay. I just heard the bad news."

"So, word has gotten out already?"

"Of course! Word travels fast, especially about someone such as Kazai. He was made a legend before he did anything...one would call... legendary."

The princess snapped, "Humph! Are you implying that his escape was my fault?"

"Of course no-"

"And what were you talking about when you said that you wanted to discuss someone's permanent suspension?" The princess interrupted.

"Well, it's like this…"

Before the doctor could finish his sentence there was a loud bang followed by several more.

"What was that?" the Princess shouted.

Dan and the other protector looked out of the window.

Dan shouted, "It appears to be coming from the Station."

"Everyone is just getting in! What could be going on over there?" The princess shouted.

Dan dashed toward the exit, "I'll go find out."

Dan didn't get very far before several hybrids began to reveal themselves within the princess' office. They came from dark corners, from behind pillars and even from the balconies. They all had the dragon foot tattoo somewhere on theirbodies. Some had strong facial features of an animal while others looked more human.

The princess' eyes widened in shock as she muttered, "Crimson Bloods."

The extremely confident doctor slowly began to walk closer to the princess, "I'm afraid that no one in this room is leaving. At least, not until there is a shifting."

The Princess stood up, "What do you mean? A Shifting?"

The doctor smiled, "A shifting in power of course. You will be shifting your power to me. Those loud explosions that you just heard were my Crimson Bloods destroying your precious station. Killing all of your unsuspecting protector Shōkans and even non-Shōkans."

The princess didn't take her eyes off of the doctor, "So, this whole time you've been working for the Crimson Bloods?" She shouted.

The doctor smiled as he gazed in the princess' eyes, "Quite the contrary... they work for me."

Chapter Seventeen

The Mode

Back in Gomorra City, the Dragon took me outside of the mansion into the courtyard. He said, "Watch me."

He took a deep breath and said, "Shōkan."

His entire body began to glow. He began radiating so much heat that the grass around him shriveled to dust. All at once his entire body caught fire. It was as if his skin and cells were all of a sudden made of fire.

"This is my FIRE MODE! In this mode, I'm faster than the human eye. In this mode, I have the strength of ten hybrids. In this mode I can defend against any attack!" The dragon slowly pointed to the sky and released a stream of light like a massive laser outlined by fire. Then, he withdrew his fire mode and was back to normal.

I looked at his clothes, and they were not damaged at all by the fire. "How is it that you can do that, but your clothes aren't even damaged?"

"Humph, I'm not sure." He took off his mask and said, "I guess that's why I was never burned by this metal mask."

Words can't possibly describe what I saw. I tried not to stare, but I couldn't look away. It wasn't until he put his mask back on that I could breathe.

"So are you going to teach me how to do that?"

"No, you could never learn to do what I just did, at least not as you are now. It takes time to master such a technique. Besides, your elements are heat and light. My elements are Fire and radiation. So, even if you were able to go into a mode, it would be completely different from mine. Your mode would probably be light mode."

"Wow, light mode. That sounds pretty cool. Yeah, I want to learn that."

The Hikari Dragon quickly said, "This isn't like that sword trick that only took you one day to learn. This technique is on a completely different level. It may take you years to master. So, what I'll do is teach you the fundamentals of the technique so that you can master it later on your own. So... are you ready?"

I nodded.

The Dragon shouted, "I said, ARE YOU READY?"

"Oh! Yes, Yes! I am ready. Sorry about that. I keep forgetting that you can't see me when I nod my head."

Back at the Umi Tribe, things were getting heated. The Crimson Bloods surrounded the collapsed protector station, and there were even a few surrounding the princess' office. As the citizens saw the hybrids surrounding the station, they began to panic. The hybrids didn't actually attack anyone, but their presence was enough to cause most of the citizens to run in fear, trying to evacuate.

Meanwhile, the princess, Dan Siratchi and Billy Woo were the only ones available to fight against a small army of hybrids.

"I can't believe this! How could you? Of all people, YOU!" Princess Tuyette shouted.

The doctor just stood there smiling as numerous Crimsons began to surround them.

The princess continued, "This doesn't make sense! You were the one that warned us about Dr. Cyrus when he was going to attack our Tribe 15 years ago! Why would you protect us then but attack us now?"

The doctor smiled, "That's just it! I couldn't allow Cyrus to destroy this Tribe! I wanted the satisfaction of doing it myself!"

Then, one of the Crimson Bloods ran towards the princess, jumping in mid-air to attack her. It was the same electric Crimson that was at the shuttle station the day Jack Findle was captured. Billy, who was standing beside the princess anticipated the Crimson's attack.

He shouted, "Shōkan!" and his left arm stretched and punched the hybrid in the stomach pushing him backward.

While still in the air, the hybrid held tightly to Billy's arm and began to exert electricity. Billy saw the lightning coming towards him so pulled back, and the water that formed his arm splashed to the ground.

Before the hybrid could land, Billy shouted, "Shōkan!" and a powerful stream of water came rushing from Billy's right hand. The hybrid flipped and dodged the stream of water and landed on his feet. The water pressure was so powerful that it cracked one of the pillars, leaving a small hole in it.

"Calm down, Bang!" Dr. Kyro shouted. "Princess Tuyette, please excuse Bang. He obviously has no control over his impulses yet. Now, as I was about to say before we were interrupted, let us discuss the Umi Tribe's surrender."

"Fool!" The princess shouted. "Do you really think that I would surrender to you and a few hybrids? I don't care if they are Crimsons: I will never surrender!"

"Princess, I don't think that you understand your current

situation. All of your reinforcements are already dead. The only way you could possibly stand a chance is if you call your father, the REAL Umi Tribe Chief."

The princess looked at the doctor with a cold stare and said, "I don't need to call my father. I have all I need to take down you and those disgusting hybrids!"

The princess looked confused, "Hold up. You've seen the power of the Umi Tribe's main branch. Why would you allow me to call for backup?"

The doctor smiled, "It's simple, defeating you is just practice. I really want to take down your father! That's the only way I can reclaim the honor of the Crimson Bloods!"

The princess continued to look confused, "The Crimson Bloods? Why would you care about their honor?" The princess shouted.

The doctor's facial expression became more serious, "I'm glad you asked. Take a seat this may take a while to explain."

Chapter Eighteen
Kyro's Past

Gomorra City, at The Hikari Dragon's Mansion
"Okay, I think I understand." I said as I was about to attempt to go into light mode again.

"Okay. First, focus my spirit energy evenly throughout my entire body. Then, summon and absorb light energy into my body and become one with it."

As I focused on going into light mode, I felt a massive amount of heat, and it happened. BOOM! It was like my body exploded.

As the steam cleared, I notice that the inside of my body was illuminating light as if my bones were glowing. "I did it! I'm a natural! I must be some kind of Shōkan prodigy!" I roared.

"No! You didn't do it!" The Dragon insisted. "I admit, you are on the right path. And the mode that you're in now may give you similar advantages to Light Mode, but it's definitely not perfected."

I was still excited, "Who cares if it's perfected if I can get the same results!"

"That's just it, you won't get the same results. As a matter of fact, if you stay that way for too long, you may damage your entire nervous system."

I immediately released my unperfected light mode, "My nervous system?"

"That's right. A perfected mode allows you to become one with your element. What you're doing is almost the opposite. You're producing light energy inside your body which will probably enhance your speed and strength, but because you are not yet one with the light, you could be fried from the inside out. Keep practicing."

I looked at the dragon and asked, "So all shōkans have a mode whether it be light, fire, water, or whatever?"

"It's possible for all shōkans to have a mode, but it's rare for normal shōkans to learn such techniques. Modes are usually reserved for elite shōkans or chiefs."

I looked up to the sky and wiped the sweat from my face and said, "Alright then! Let's do this."

Back in the Umi Tribe, at The Princess' office.

Doctor Kyro signaled the hybrids, "Crimsons! Fall back for now. I wish to tell the princess a story before I lay her and this tribe to rest."

The hybrids began to back up and some even sat down. The princess glared at the doctor with a deadly stare. Dan and Billy observed their surroundings as if they were trying to formulate some sort of plan.

Dr. Kyro began to pace the floor, "It all began about forty years ago. There was a little hybrid boy. For a hybrid, he had very strong human features. The only thing that made him look like a hybrid was the top of his head. See, instead of hair on his head he had scales. The hybrid boy had no home and no parents so he traveled from town to town, from city to city. He found that not only did the animals fear him, but the humans did too and he had no idea why. The little boy only wanted a friend or better yet, a family. You know, people that he could relate to."

The doctor stopped pacing as he continued, "Then, the boy stumbled into this very land. He found other hybrids, humanoids in fact. At first he was happy. But, that happiness soon turned into sorrow when he realized that they didn't accept him either because he looked too much like a human. But one day, the boy made a friend, it was a fellow hybrid. They played together everyday since the very first day they met."

Kyro smirked, "That's how the boy found out that he had

elemental abilities. His friend was the one that made him realize who he was, a Crimson Blood. Their bond was like no other. To show their appreciation for one another, the two hybrids agreed to exchange gifts. Neither of them had money, so they used whatever resources they had to obtain their gifts. The little hybrid boy stole a hat for his friend. To impress his friend, he wore the hat, but when he arrived to meet his friend, he saw that Umi Tribe protectors had gotten there first and slaughtered him."

Kyro's face was filled with malice as he continued, "One of the protectors came towards the little hybrid boy. The little hybrid was so frightened that he couldn't move."

The protector said to the little boy, "You're lucky kid. We just defeated some hybrids in the same direction you're heading. Who knows what they would have done to you if we didn't get here before you."

"The little hybrid was mistaken for a human, all because of the hat he had stolen for his friend. Although his life was spared, the little boy's heart was forever broken…again."

"As the boy got older he saw more and more of these kinds of killings. He was always able to escape as long as he was wearing what he then called his lucky hat."

The princess interrupted, "So let me guess, you're that little boy hybrid? And the hair on your head is a wig?"

Kyro snarled, "Spoiler Alert! For goodness sake Tuyette! Where's your class? Am I not the one telling the story?"

Then, there was a pause.

"Can I continue now? Or do you have any more questions?" Kyro asked. The princess just glared at Kyro. "I'll take that as a yes."

"Now, as I was saying before I was so rudely interrupted: As I got older I found that there were many advantages to pretending to be human. I didn't have to sneak around all of the time. I wasn't chased away by locals or even seen as a monster."

Kyro began to smile a little as he continued, "So, the first thing that I did was find a wig, something that I could wear at all times. Then, I went to school, right here in the Umi Tribe; I was always quite crafty. Before enrolling myself into school I found the records of someone who had died. I removed their certificate of death from the records and borrowed their name. Well, to be more accurate, I stole their name. And, to be honest, I don't even remember what my real name is anymore, that is, if I ever had one."

There was a pause as Kyro stared off into space, as if he were trying to remember.

Then he snapped back into reality and continued, "Anyway, I did all of this because I wanted the opportunity to find the shōkan that killed my friend so that I could kill him. My original plan was to become a protector, but I could see that hiding my abilities as a Crimson Blood would have been nearly impossible. So, I decided to do something that did not require showing my physical attributes. That's why I became a scientist."

"Surprisingly, I was exceptionally good in science. Because of that Dr. Cyrus gave me an internship which eventually became a job. When Dr. Cyrus became the lead scientist, I remained his top assistant. He showed me many things related to human biology and even human morale."

"He showed me just how cruel the shōkans of the Umi Tribe were. The more I worked with him the deeper my hate grew for him and this wretched Tribe! Then, I realized that Dr. Cyrus hated the Umi Tribe just as much as I did. So, my hate toward him became more bearable. I found that Dr. Cyrus and I had many things in common but our ambitions were very different."

"He felt that he deserved to be the Tribe Chief because of his knowledge and all of his great accomplishments. He hated that a barbaric tribe such as this one would not even consider electing a scientist as chief, not even in a thousand years. His simple annoyance slowly grew into an obsession."

The doctor smiled as if he was proud of himself, "I can't say that I didn't play a part in him going mad. See, every time that he would vent to me about your father, I instigated, just feeding his anger. Before long, he had a bright idea to overthrow the entire Umi Tribe, including your father's underwater fortress. I have to admit, if I hadn't revealed it to the Chief myself, his plan may have worked. But, instead of letting him go through with it, I had my own objective. I wanted to be the one to take down this tribe. I wanted to be the one to take down this tribe of murderers."

"But that's not the only reason I snitched: I understood that if Dr. Cyrus' plan failed he would be executed along with me. I also knew that if I snitched, I would probably get his job as lead scientist, which would put me in a better position to take out the Umi Tribe myself."

"This should show you how twisted and corrupt your society is! But, anyway, Dr. Cyrus created a formula that was capable of transforming harmless animoid hybrids into gargantuan hybrids unlike anything that the world has seen before, turning small puppy-sized animoids into monsters the size of a skyscrapers."

"His flaw was that his animoids had the intelligence of mold and that gargantuan hybrids are nothing more than big targets. But, his final flaw was that he trusted me."

"Speaking of trust…I gained so much trust from your father when I told him about Dr. Cyrus. That's why I was promoted. Anyway, Your father…your father was smart, he wasn't as nearly as foolish as you Tuyette."

The princess just glared at Kyro.

Kyro continued, "Your father almost immediately called the other Tribes for backup, unlike you, Princess. But anyway, the Hikari Tribe Chief even showed up to help. With the three Shōkan tribes working together Dr. Cyrus' plan quickly died, and so did he. In all of the confusion of the war, I was able to find that shōkan that killed my friend and I killed him. I made it look like he was just another victim of the war."

The doctor paused. "What happened after the war ended fueled my hate even more toward your Tribe, especially your father. At the time, I didn't realize that the Hikari Tribe didn't have the same policy as the Umi Tribe. They don't kill all hybrids; they just killed hybrids that posed a threat.

"This caused your father to blame them for Dr. Cyrus' collection of animoids but the Hikari Tribe had nothing to do with it. It was me: I had to capture them myself. I was forced to capture my own kind and run experiments on them! Most of them died."

Kyro paused and looked away. He took a deep breath and continued.

"So, your father, the extremist that he is, decided to wipe out every hybrid in the world, especially Crimson Bloods because of their strength. He traveled from place to place, killing hybrids on sight. Then, when an organized group of

Crimson Bloods came together to stop him, he went and got help from the Shido Tribe. With their combined strength, your father is responsible for the extinction of the Crimson Bloods--my family."

The princess looked around her, "As far as I can see, there are plenty of Crimson Bloods here!"

"Don't be naïve, Princess. These Crimsons aren't natural. That would be impossible! They are all my creations. You see, I used my own blood to make them the way they are now." Kyro said proudly.

"After Dr. Cyrus died, I began running studies on myself and after witnessing all of the great abilities of the Shōkans during the war, I decided to exercise my capabilities. Studies in my DNA showed that I have multiple dragons in my bloodline. When I learned this, I was able to unlock four elements. That day was the day I realized that I am the only one born to destroy the Umi Tribe."

"You don't say...why is that?" The princess sarcastically interrupted.

"Because, all of my abilities trump all of the Umi Tribe abilities!" Kyro shouted viciously.

"What might they be?" The princess asked calmly.

"You'll find out soon enough. Now, as I was saying... Once

I knew my elemental abilities, I knew that I was destined to overthrow this place. But, I knew that no matter how strong I became I couldn't do it alone."

"Then, one day, I was just walking through town and noticed a young man. His eyes reminded me of my own--not physically of course, it was deeper than that. He had eyes of loneliness, just like mine."

"So, I approached him and offered him companionship and power. After that, I found others just like him and convinced them to join me. Then, using my own blood I was able to create the formula that produces what you see before you. I even gave them each a specific element of choice."

Kyro smiled and looked at the princess, "Impressive, right?"

There was a pause of silence.

Kyro smirked and said, "I'm surprised! Don't you have anything to say, Princess?"

The princess held her head down and paused. Then she looked directly in the eyes of Kyro and said, "Yes, I do have something that I'd like to say."

Kyro looked surprised and said, "Okay, spit it out!"

The princess looked to her left and then to her right. Then she looked at Kyro and said, "SHŌKAN!"

At that moment, the princess stretched out her arms and released ten thin yet extremely powerful streams of water from the tips of her fingers. Dan and Billy both ducked in order to make sure the princess hit her targets. She aimed for all of the hybrids on the balcony and one that was behind Dan. The princess' one attack took out six of the nine hybrids there (excluding Kyro).

Each stream of water punctured through each of the princess' targets leaving a hole in their bodies.

As the Crimsons began to fall, the princess continued her assault. She aimed her jetstream at the remaining Crimson Bloods, but they all dodged her attacks. The princess, then, felt a massive wave of heat quickly growing closer. She instinctively jumped out of the way just in time to be out of reach from the fire exhorted from Kyro's mouth.

The princess thought to herself, "Fire, huh? That's one of his elements. Three more to go."

Billy immediately shouted, "SHŌKAN!" He attempted to become a giant using cell manipulation, but in the midst of his attack, Bang snuck up from behind and electrocuted Billy, leaving him unconscious, face down in the water that he summoned.

Then Bang, along with two other Crimsons, began to surround Dan Siratchi. Dan calmly reached for his two swords.

Kyro slowly walked toward the princess. "I must admit, that was quite impressive, Princess. I've always heard that your jetstream was powerful, but I never thought that it would pierce so easily through the body of a Crimson. On top of that, you took down six of them at one time. However, it doesn't really matter now."

"And why is that?" Tuyette snarled.

Kyro stood in confidence, "Because now you have to face me! But, because of our history, I'll give you one last chance to call your father for help." Kyro said while slowly removing his jacket and his wig revealing his head to be bald and covered with scales.

Chapter Nineteen

Umi Strong

Meanwhile, Herona and Chief Kazan were riding a shuttle just a few cities away from the Umi Tribe. As they were riding, the shuttle began to unexpectedly slow down. All of the normal civilians began to complain and wonder what was going on. Herona and Kazan, along with a few others were on the private section of the shuttle, became confused, too.

Then the shuttle's intercom sounded: "This is your conductor speaking. Our next stop will be Mum's Village. I know that this is not your scheduled destination, but we just received word that there is some kind of disaster ahead. Currently, we do not have any details about the situation or even what town it's in. A radio broadcast will be airing in the next thirty minutes, and they promise to have all of the major details, including what's holding us up and which city it's in. By then, we will have arrived in safely at Mums Village. Please don't ask our staff any questions about the current situation because we are ALL in the dark just as you are. Thank you in advance for your patience and understanding."

All of the people on the shuttle were outraged. Some people took out their radios while others just began shouting and complaining about having to wait. Others began complaining to the staff and asking them questions about the situation.

Herona and Kazan both looked at each other. Herona said, "You don't think..."

Kazan said, "I don't know, all we can do now is just wait." Then Kazan smiled to make Herona feel at ease, "I wouldn't worry. It's not like we can do anything about it now anyway."

Herona looked out of the window as the sun was beginning to go down, "You know what...you're right."

In Gomorra City, I was still trying to learn the basis of light mode to no avail. "I've been doing this all day! Why can't I get this?" I shouted.

"I already told you! This is not something that you could just learn in a day. It could take years."

I sat down on the ground, "It feels like I'm getting nowhere."

The Hikari Dragon smirked and said, "You're wrong."

"What do you mean?"

"This whole time, all you have been doing is practicing

control."

"So, what is that supposed to mean?" I asked.

"It means that now you should have more control with your abilities."

"What do you mean, more control?"

"It's not astral science! I mean exactly what I said! You'll have better control. When you summon heat to your sword it won't be so sloppy anymore. When releasing a light beam, your accuracy in controlling the size, heat, and pressure will now be more efficient! All because you've been trying to go into light mode which requires you to constantly focus all of the energy in your body."

"Ohhhh, I get it now."

"Were you toying with me?"

I just smiled and laughed. Seconds later, Porsha came running toward us. "Master, Master Dragon! Kazai isn't a liar after all!"

We both looked confused.

"What are you talking about?" The dragon said.

Porsha looked directly at me, "I just heard some people

in the city talking. They said that the Umi Tribe is being attacked right now by Crimson Bloods!"

My heart dropped. I thought about my mother. Tears almost formed in my eyes. But when I thought about Dan I knew that he would protect her. Then I thought about all of the people I've met since becoming a protector-- Princess Tuyette, Juicy, Master Kim Lee, Broadie, and even Steve. I slowly began to panic.

"I have to go!" I shouted.

"Don't be hasty! You don't even know if this is true or just some rumor." The dragon persisted.

Porsha stepped forward, "I also heard that the official news-cast is going to air on the radio in just a few minutes. Some reporters are on the way to the Umi Tribe to check it out." I looked at the dragon, "We have to go there and help!"

The dragon raised his left eyebrow, "We? I don't have to do anything but eat crap and die. I'm not getting involved in that!"

"What? Why not?"

"For one, no one asked me to. Secondly, I'm an exile. Third, it's not a paying job. Fourth, Gomorra City pays me to stay here in the city!"

"This is not a time to be joking! We need to go now!"

"KAZAI!"

I looked at the Hikari Dragon.

He said, "Look in my eyes, I am serious."

I said, "No way, you're not the type to be all about money, are you? You even trained me and didn't once mention money."

"I said that I would train you, I never said that I would do it for free!" The dragon said as he folded his armed.

I just looked at him as he continued. "You ate my food, slept in my house, and received two days of my training! You should've known that wasn't free!"

I thought that he actually cared, but he was all about money. I turned around and focused my energy. I entered into my unperfected light mode. Then, I turned to the Hikari Dragon, "I guess that's what I get for assuming that you were a decent man. I should have known, you were exiled after all. I'll pay you for training me after I go save and my Tribe."

The dragon coldly responded, "You should know kid, nothing in this world is free. You owe me twenty-thousand dollars!"

Then I turned to Porsha, "Give me your sword!"

She looked at me in disgust, "NO!!!"

The dragon spoke up, "Just give him your sword! If he doesn't bring it back, I'll just add it to his bill."

She unstrapped her sheath and tossed it to me.

Once I had the sword I ran toward the Umi Tribe as fast as I could. Before I knew it I was out of Gomorra City and on the path back to the Umi Tribe. Even though my light-mode was unperfected and I was advised not to use it, I did it anyway and it allowed me to run ten times faster than I could before. I felt like a brand new person. I moved so fast that time itself seemed to slow down for me.

Back at the Umi Tribe, the princess was facing off against Kyro while Dan was facing off against three Crimsons, all at once.

Kyro looked to the princess, "Last chance princess. What is it going to be? Are you going to call the Umi Tribe Chief for backup or will you surrender?"

The princess took a slow deep breath as she thought to herself, 'He's basically begging me to call for backup. What is he planning? Whatever it is, I won't fall for it!'

"I won't surrender or call my father! But I will fight!" The princess shouted as she ripped off her skirt in order to get it out of the way, revealing her tights that perfectly matched her form-fitting turquoise shirt and golden blouse .

Kyro said, "Oh my, Princess, how sexy."

"Shut your face!" Princess Tuyette shouted as she ran toward Kyro.

"You're fast!" Kyro said before spitting several streams of fire at her. The princess dodged every attack.

The princess came face to face with Kyro and was on the assault. She punched and kicked, but Kyro maneuvered past every swing. His movements were similar to a snake.

Meanwhile, the other Crimsons were surrounding Dan Siratchi. Dan pulled out his blades as two of the three crimsons did the same. The other Crimson named Bang began exhorting electricity from his body.

The two Crimsons with swords attacked Dan. He was able to dodge their sword thrusts, but Bang came at him from behind. Dan anticipated Bang's sneak attack.

What the Crimsons didn't know was that Dan's swords were special. Dan's swords were called whip-blades because they could change from a solid slicing sword into a metal whip that could easily be extended or retracted. Dan's blades were even more effective than a normal whip-blade because he could detach them from the handle at any time and add a new one from his arsenal.

As Bang tried to sneak-attack Dan from behind, Dan whipped his blade at one of the other Crimsons, and it wrapped around that Crimson's sword and its entire arm. Dan pulled the hybrid in Bang's direction, causing Bang to be stabbed in the chest and the other Crimson to be shocked by Bang's electricity all while avoiding the other hybrid.

Bang quickly stood up and said, "That was only a scratch."

Then, Dan retracted his blade from the unconscious hybrid. Dan realized that his blade wasn't very effective in comparison to Bang's electricity. The hybrid only had small scratches on his arm when the blade should have nearly ripped his arm off.

Dan sighed, "Well, that's one down."

Bang and the other Crimson, then, attacked Dan simultaneously. Bang shot an electrical current from his arm while the other Crimson spat lava from his mouth. Dan ducked and maneuvered while whipping his blades at the feet of both Crimsons. His blades wrapped around the legs of both Crimsons, and he swept them off of their feet. The lava-spitting Crimson fell backward and was burned in the face by his own lava. He shouted, "MY EYES! Ah my EYES!"

When Bang fell back he looked up at Dan and smiled. Then, he released a massive wave of electricity through Dan's blade. Dan stayed calm and touched his two blades together. The lava spitting Crimson was immediately electrocuted by Bang's attack.

Dan said, "The handles to my swords are impervious to electrical currents but the blades aren't. Simple safety measure for situations like this." Then Dan retracted his blades.

Bang attempted to stand up but couldn't move. "Why can't I move?" Bang shouted. Then he noticed about a dozen tiny needles sticking out of his body.

"Are these paralyzing needles?" Bang asked.

Dan gave Bang a cold stare, "No, they are poison needles. Once your body is immobilized that's when you know you're about to die."

"What? I don't want to die!" Bang shouted.

"That's interesting: you want to kill and yet you haven't considered the possibility that you would be killed."

"But when did you? You had both swords in your hands?"

"Well, because it's your dying wish, I'll tell you–"

At that moment, Dan was interrupted by a Crimson that was plunged through the glass window from outside. Dan, Tuyette, and Kyro turned to see a falling Crimson with horns land on its head from about thirty-six feet in the air.

Standing in the window sill was Master Kim Lee. He shouted, "It's good to see that you're okay, Princess! My old friends and I are taking out the trash! Do you need any assistance in there?"

The Princess smiled, "No, thanks! I'm about to wrap things up here myself! How are the others?"

Master Kim Lee smiled, "They're in that place that we discussed earlier, they followed that procedure that your father put in place."

The princess smiled and nodded as Master Kim Lee continued, "Although they all survived, some were injured. But, they won't be able to get back here for a while! I was the only one who was able to escape without using that tactic so I gathered my old retired buddies, and we got to work."

Then, someone screamed for Master Kim Lee and he said, "Gotta go!" as he ran off back into the battlefield.

Kyro gripped his fists. The Princess looked at Dan, "Dan! Are you finished over there?"

Dan looked at Bang's dead body and nodded. The princess said, "I want you to go outside and help take down the rest of those wannabe Crimsons!"

Dan began to run towards the broken window but he stopped and turned to Tuyette, "Princess! Please don't underestimate Kyro; I've analyzed what he said about having four elemental abilities. He said that all of the Crimsons got their powers from his blood. If that's true, then he doesn't just have four elemental abilities he has at least five. Remember, Jack Findle has Ice. One of the Crimsons that Kazai fought used toxic smoke and the two I fought had lava and electricity. And as you know, Kyro himself was just breathing fire. That means he has five elemental abilities, not four. Also, consider that, although the other Crimsons were just counterfeits, he's the real deal."

The princess rolled her eyes, "You don't think I've already figured that out! Go share that intelligence with the people who need it!" Dan nodded, jumped out of the window and entered the battlefield.

The princess turned to Kyro, "You've underestimated the Umi Tribe! That was your downfall."

Kyro began to laugh, "Why are you looking so confident all of a sudden? So what, he figured out my bluff. All that did was make your death less interesting."

"You're forgetting that your attack on my protectors, the UMI TRIBE PROTECTORS was a fail! All of my troops are still alive and yours are dying as we speak!"

"I wouldn't be so sure about that." Kyro said.

All of a sudden there was a beeping sound like an alarm going off. Kyro pulled a watch from his pocket and pressed a button to stop the beeping.

He said, "It won't be long now. Just look out the window, I promise I won't attack you. Besides when I kill you, I don't want you to have any excuses."

The princess hesitated but walked over to the window without turning from Kyro. Then she heard a voice cry, "RE-TREAT!"

She looked to Kyro, "You son of a...."

Chapter Twenty

Explosion

Moments Earlier:
The retired veterans were keeping the remaining citizens of the Umi Tribe safe from the Crimson Bloods.

At first, the veterans had the upper hand because of their seasoned skills and experience. Master Kim Lee easily assessed the Crimson's powers, which would normally trump their own-- that is when it comes to summoning water--but the veterans had more up their sleeves than basic water tricks. The veterans mastered many elements of the ocean besides water: some mastered salt, others mastered sand and some even mastered ice.

So, after analyzing their situation, Master Kim Lee lead the assault against the Crimson Bloods. The old man from the induction ceremony was there. He summoned a dome made from salt in order to protect a group of orphaned children. The dome was summoned from underground so that it would have a solid foundation. The dome was taller than it was round so that they would have plenty of air. The old man then used the dome to attack multiple Crimsons at a time by creating temporary openings in the dome and then shooting sharp shards of salt from the openings.

Another old man stood from a tall building, summoning massive ice glaciers and dropping them on the crimsons. One of the old women stayed out of sight and summoned ocean water to hit the Crimsons that emitted electricity. A group of the veterans who'd mastered sand summoned a quicksand trap, taking out many Crimsons all at once.

Everything was going according to plan until just moments after Dan Siratchi came to the battlefield to help them. Then everything exploded… literally.

Master Kim Lee saw Dan, "So, you've come to back us up, huh?"

"Right! Well, based on what I've seen so far, you guys already know not to use water against them right?" Dan said while tripping one of the crimsons using his whip-blade.

"That's right!" Kim Lee said as he shot a shard of salt from his hand like a dagger.

Then, without warning, all of the remaining Crimsons began to grow. The crimsons that were stabbed grew until the hole in their body looked like a scratch. Some of the Crimsons that were trapped in ice easily broke free. The Crimsons that were trapped in the quicksand escaped by merely stepping out. The only Crimsons that didn't pose a threat were the ones that were already dead.

All of the veterans were confused.

One cried out, "What's going on? Are they getting bigger or am I now rapidly shrinking?"

"Crap, I must have forgotten to take my medicine!"

"This is like that war, all over again! Run away! RETREAT!"

Master Kim Lee looked at Dan and said, "Go back with the princess!"

Dan shouted, "Why?"

Kim Lee said, "Because you're bad luck! None of this happened until you showed up!"

The Crimsons became even more aggressive than before and gained a great boost in energy and strength. Some of them began to attack buildings and structures as if they wanted to show off their newfound power. The old man's salt dome suddenly went from being impenetrable to being in one of the most vulnerable places on the battlefield. Many Crimsons flocked to his dome and attacked it at once.

In order to keep it from collapsing completely, he had to constantly summon more salt as they hit it. The old man on the roof was now in reach of the Crimsons. All of a sudden he was vulnerable. Luckily, the old woman who was hiding remained hidden as she began to shake in fear.

Meanwhile, the princess gazed out the window at her city being destroyed. "This is just like the war against Dr. Cyrus." Tuyette said as she slowly turned to Kyro.

"Not exactly. Dr. Cyrus created gargantuan hybrids which were pretty much just big targets, and they were created from animoids. My giants aren't as big as Dr. Cyrus' army, but they are smarter and more powerful because they are Crimson Bloods. Besides, Dr. Cyrus never actually made it into the city. He barely made it onto the beach. My Crimsons, however, are right in the heart of your precious town. So, don't compare me!" Kyro shouted with malice.

"I'm done talking. I'm going to take you out and go help my people." The princess said with great determination.

"You better worry about yourself, Princess! Otherwise you'll find yourself dead!"

"How can someone find themselves dead? Besides, didn't I say I was done talking?" The princess said before running toward Kyro.

Kyro jumped back vertically and landed on the balcony. "Face it, Princess: you don't have a chance! Your life is in my hands now! The only thing you can attack me with is that Jetstream of yours. If you use it, I'll just counter with lightning. You'll instantly be electrocuted. Don't forget, I am not like Bang. Although he was powerful, my lightning is ten times stronger than his!"

"Then come down here and fight me!" The princess shouted.

"I'm smarter than you, Princess. I know to keep my distance if you get too close then my lightning won't matter, just like those six of my Crimsons that you—"

The princess jumped and in an instance her fist was embedded in Kyro's face.

The impact sent him flying through the wall into the lobby area, which did not have a second level. Despite being punched through a wall down to the first level, Kyro landed on his feet with one knee to the ground.

"I admit, you caught me off guard. I had no idea that you could do that." Kyro said as he wiped his face and slowly stood up while dusting off. "Please enlighten me. How did you do that?"

The princess jumped down from the hole in the wall. As she was about to touch the floor, she remained in the air and then landed softly.
Kyro's eyes widened, "So, that's it! I've never even considered that to even be a possibility. Wind, the Umi Tribe can summon wind. That's why. That's why your Jetstream is so

powerful; it's amplified with wind power. So, it's true what they say."

The princess slowly began to step forward.

Kyro continued, "Every Tribe really does have their secret techniques. The fact that you are willing to reveal it to me tells me something. Either you actually plan to kill me or you've been backed into a corner, and you have no other alternatives."

The princess jumped toward Kyro. "Shōkan!" She said as she used the wind around her to amplify her speed. She tried to punch Kyro again, but he quickly dodged. Tuyette quickly re-adjusted and punched Kyro. This time he barely budged. Tuyette was shocked.

"Is that all? I expected more from the great Umi Tribe!" Kyro shouted as he began to exhort a massive amount of lightning from his body. Tuyette flew back just in time.

Kyro began laughing, "So what if you have wind now! That doesn't change anything! Your wind only trumps two possibly three of my five abilities."

"This isn't a card game, Kyro! The one who wins today won't be because of the amount of abilities they have. It'll be because of how strong a single ability is!" The princess said boldly.

Tuyette's entire body began to shake rapidly. "Are you getting scared?" Kyro shouted.

"No, I'm getting prepared!" Tuyette said as she closed her eyes. Wind began to blow all directions from her body.

"You think I'm just going to let you prepare to attack me!" Kyro said as he shot a bolt of electricity at her. The electricity was deflected by the wind. "The wind is protecting her?" Kyro said under his breathe.

Then, all of the wind from Tuyette's body began to blow in one direction, upward. Tuyette opened her eyes and said, "Now, I'm ready."

Tuyette flew toward Kyro so fast that by the time he saw her coming he had already been punched.

He thought, "She's even faster than before."

Kyro began to exert lightning from his entire body thinking that she would not be able to touch him or even get close to him. Tuyette's wind deflected all of the lightning that came her way as she attacked him. Tuyette's body moved so rapidly that when she missed one of her punches, the momentum of her own force sent her flying. When this happened she was able to adjust quickly.

It didn't take long for Kyro to see that if he wanted to survive, he would have to give it his all. So, he began using his lightning to move faster.

Once Tuyette realized that Kyro's speed had increased as well she began to attack with a wind slicing technique. She used her hands and feet to send powerful currents of wind that sliced through anything in its path.

She attacked Kyro from all directions but to no avail. He dodged everything and what he couldn't dodge he blocked using lighting. As Tuyette chopped and kicked she sliced her lobby apart. As the blade-like wind current missed Kyro it was hitting every wall in the room so hard that from the outside it looked like there were several, thin mini explosions coming through the building.

Kyro thought to himself, 'This must be her mode…her wind-mode. If this is a mode then that means she can't stay this way for very long. Which is good for me because I don't know how much longer I can keep up.'

Tuyette thought to herself, 'I can't last much longer like this. I have to take him down NOW!'

At that moment, Tuyette quickly jumped backward away from Kyro. She flipped back, landing on her hands, and she began to spin emitting a massive, slicing wind-current in every direction from her legs at waist level. The wind quickly attacked Kyro, but he was able to dodge it at the last second by jumping over the current.

As he was about to land another wind current was coming for his face, so he used his lightning to cancel it out at the last second.

Kyro thought, 'That was close!' Then, he looked where Tuyette was spinning, but she was gone. He looked on both sides and behind him and didn't see her.

Then, he looked up to see Tuyette speeding toward him. She chopped through the air, sending one last slicing wind-current from her arm. Kyro attempted to dodge but didn't have enough time. He tried exerting lightning, but the wind was too fast. So, he held up his left arm to block, and the wind current sliced through his arm, almost cutting it all the way through; but, Kyro manage to cancel out some of the impact with his lightning. Kyro screamed as lightning exhorted from his body hitting Tuyette who was no longer surrounded by wind.

She went flying through the front entrance, tearing down the front half of the already destroyed lobby. She landed across the street with her back leaning on the front door of one of the local businesses.

Kyro continued to scream as he ripped off what was left of his arm. He began to walk through the rubble towards the unconscious Tuyette. Kyro held up his right hand exhorting more lightning than before, "You stole my arm from me! You, you, I will kill you! You b—"

All of a sudden, Kyro fell face first to the ground. He sat up and looked at his feet to see Dan's whip-blades wrapped around his ankles.

Kyro instinctively turned and blew a cloud of ice at Dan. Leaning backwards Dan managed to dodge most of the freezing cloud but his hands barely got caught in the ice, freezing them.

When Kyro saw this he quickly grabbed the blades and pulled them, throwing Dan Siratchi twenty yards into the same spot as Tuyette. Dan landed upside down on the back of his neck. Dan looked at Kyro, who from his perspective was upside down and blurry. Kyro was exerting lightning from his right hand again.

As Kyro walked toward them the lightning from his hand began ripping into the ground as if the lightning itself couldn't wait to attack them. Kyro stood on the other side of the street and looked at both of them, "I'm going to kill both of you in one shot!" Kyro's lightning covered his entire body.

Then, he released it all from his right hand pointed directly at Tuyette and Dan Siratchi. There was a huge explosion leaving a huge cloud of smoke and dust.

Kyro walked toward his targets. He looked and to his surprise both of them were gone. Kyro thought, 'I know I didn't disintegrate them. Where are their bodies?' Then he became angrier and began to shout, "Where are their bodies?

Where? Where are you hiding, Princess?"

As the smoke began to clear, Kyro saw a figure standing. The more the smoke cleared, the more he was able to recognize the figure. The man was holding Dan on his shoulders and Princess Tuyette in his arms.

Dan said, "Nice timing."

The princess began to wake up. She looked up at the figure and said, "Kazai?"

When Kyro got a good look at the person holding his victims, he said, "So, you've come back."

There I stood holding the woman who had me imprisoned and the man who said that it was my own fault. I slowly and carefully began to put both of them down.

Tuyette said, "Kazai, I know what you're thinking! You can't do it: you have to get away now!"

Dan agreed, "She right. You have to get out of here!"

After I sat them down, I asked Dan, "Where's my mother?"

Dan said, "She's safe; she was out of town when this all started. In fact, she left to go get your real father so that he could help you out of jail."

I felt a great relief. I couldn't say anything, so I just smiled. Then, I turned to Kyro and walked toward him.

Dan tried to get up but couldn't.

Kyro shouted, "So, he returns. Do you really think that you alone will make a difference?"

I reached for my blade and said, "Well, I am the Umi Tribe's trump card."

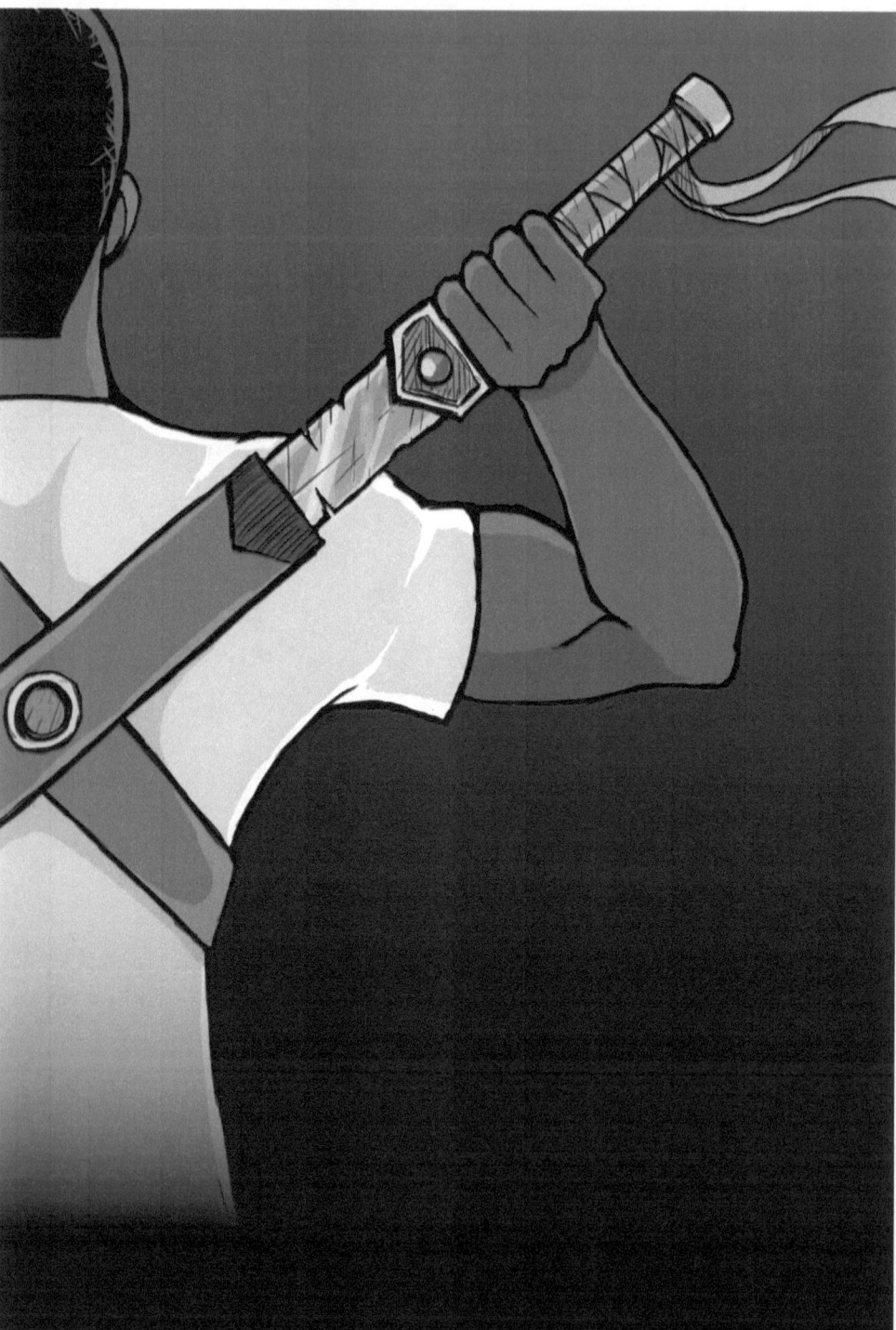

Chapter Twenty One
Kazai Returns

Now that the Crimson Bloods had the upper hand, Master Kim Lee changed his strategy. Instead of attacking he decided that it would be best to defend, protect and rescue. He ordered all of the salt-element shōkans to create more protective domes. Then, as Master Kim Lee distracted the now Giant Crimsons so that the others could safely enter the domes. Two or more shōkans were inside the domes constantly reinforcing them.

Things were looking bad, but since I arrived, I had confidence that I would make a difference.

Dan grabbed my ankle, "Wait! That's Dr. Kyro, he's a Crimson."

"What? Dr. Kyro? I knew that he created the Crimsons Bloods, but I never thought that he would be one himself? What else should I know?"

"He has five elemental abilities: lava, fire, ice, electricity and toxic smoke."

"Thanks" I said as I walked forward toward Kyro.

As I walked closer, Kyro thought to himself, 'Between my missing arm and his Hikari bloodline this might be difficult. My Lightning, Fire and Lava all would be useless against someone like him. On the bright side, all he can do is apply heat to his sword. It was a good call keeping him from finding a master.'

I didn't hesitate. "Shōkan." I said as I pulled out my blade.

From a distance, I swung my sword at Kyro. He didn't see it coming at first, but at the very last second he dodged my wave of condensed heat and light.

He looked at me in shock as he thought to himself, 'I had no idea that he could do that! He must have figured out how to use his power. In that case, I'm going to have to change tactics!'

I swung my blade as I began to run toward him, sending multiple waves all at once. He managed to dodge them while keeping his distance. His movements were unlike anything that I'd ever seen. He was able to dodge my attacks by twisting and flipping his body in mid-air.

As my attacks missed him, they hit several buildings, scarring and blasting holes into them. I thought to myself, 'This isn't working. I need to trap him.'

So, I began to focus all of my attacks lower to the ground making it harder for Kyro to dodge. That way, when he jumped I could time the next attack to slice his legs as he landed.

To my surprise, Kyro continued to dodge, although he was no longer able to keep his distance. That's when my plan "B" kicked in. The entire time I was also aiming my attacks at a standing wall from a collapsed building. The wall began to fall toward Kyro.

Kyro looked up and instinctively held up his left arm--the one that has been sliced by the Princess. Electricity emerged from it, and he stopped the wall from falling on him. But, just as he did, I used that opportunity to hit him with another attack.

As I jumped toward with my blade, lightning erupted from his body and destroyed the wall. The impact of the blast canceled my attack and prevented me from getting any closer. Some of the debris even hit me in the face.

As he stood there in rubble and diminishing clouds of dust. He looked at his left arm as the lightning emerged from it, I began to catch my breath.

Then, he smiled, "I admit, that was clever. You almost got me. But, it seems that although your waves of heat are strong, they aren't as strong as my lightning. Which means that even if you managed to hit me with it I could just use my lightning to cancel it out. Face it, Kid! Whatever advantage that you thought you had doesn't even matter anymore!"

I thought to myself, 'He's right, my attacks are useless now. Unless, I switch from long-range attacks and…yeah, that's what I'll do.'

Before I could move, Kyro sent a stream of lightning straight at me from his left arm. The lightning looked like a hand extending toward me. To my surprise, it didn't hit me but grabbed my sword instead.

Then, I felt my blade pulling away from me. 'Is this a magnetic charge?' I thought as I gripped my sword tighter.

Kyro shouted, "Without your sword you don't have a chance in beating me!" I held onto my sword as tightly as I could. The magnetic charge was so powerful that it began to pull my entire body. I began using both hands to hold on and planted my feet firmly on the ground, yet my body was still slowly being pulled towards Kyro.

Dan shouted, "Kazai! Momentum!"

I knew exactly what Dan meant. He was suggesting that I use Kyro's Magnetic Charge against him and allow myself to be pulled so that I can stab him, but before I could do anything, Kyro used his right hand and sent a bolt of lightning at Dan Siratchi.

I, instinctively, let go of the sword and ran as fast I could in order to protect Dan. My sword, still charged with lightning, went flying into the battlefield and stabbed into one of the Giant Crimsons.

I was too late. Dan was hit before I could get there.

Kyro laughed, "Ha, Got 'eem!"

I knelt down and began to shake Dan's non-responsive body. Princess Tuyette had a determined look on her face as she attempted to stand up but could barely move.

"Dan! Wake up! WAKE UP! PLEASE!"

Kyro's laughter grew louder, "Face it, Kid! He's dead!"

I stood up, "You're wrong. It's not over! In fact, it's just begun."

Kyro snarled, "So, you're resorting to bluffing now! Not your best weapon b—"

I interrupted, "SHŌKAN!" My entire body began to glow internally as I attempted to go into light-mode, despite everything in me telling me not to.

Chapter Twenty Two
Light Mode

I turned to Kyro who was frozen in awe.

"YAH!" I shouted as I flew toward Kyro in one stride. He tried to emit lightning from his body, but it was too late, I was too fast. I punched Kyro directly in the face. Kyro's resistance was strong, but the impact of my punch was stronger. It was so great that it sent him flying into and through a building.

"Amazing," said the awe-filled princess.

I raced to Kyro so that he wouldn't have a chance to recover before my next attack. Before I could see him or reach him, through the rubble I saw a blast of lightning coming straight for me. It was like everything was moving in slow motion, which made it easy for me to dodge the lightning. As I followed the lightning to it's source, I grabbed one of the flying rocks from debris and mushed it into Kyro's face breaking the rock and sending him flying again.

This time, his body was spinning in the air, doing involuntary cartwheels. Kyro twisted his body while emitting lightning to the ground in mid air. With the force of the lightning, he managed to land on his feet.

When he landed, I was right there to meet him with a kick, which would have sent him flying again, but, thanks to the my newfound speed, I was able to run past him and stop him with a punch and again with a knee. In an instance, I was hitting him with a barrage of kicks and punches.

Before long, Kyro had fallen to his knees. He was short of breath and bleeding from his mouth. I knew that it was time for me to take him down once and for all. Then, just as I was rushing toward Kyro in attempt to finish him, a sharp pain jumped through my legs.

"AHHH!!" I shouted as I stumbled due to my momentum.

As I fell, it was like I could clearly hear The Hikari Dragon's voice warning me about using the unperfected light mode. The pain was inconceivable; it was like every nerve in my legs was on fire.

"It looks like that form of yours has its side effects." Kyro said as he spat blood from his mouth.

He tried to stand up but couldn't. I could barely stand myself. I began to feel sporadic, sharp flashes of pain throughout my body. I fell to my knees and release the unperfected light mode.

When Kyro saw this, he mustered up the strength to stand up and kicked me in the face. When I fell, he immediately continued kicking me. Then, he kicked me so hard that I went flying, crashing to the trunk of a tree then to the ground.

The Princess shouted, "GET UP!"

As I tried to get up, I felt sharp pains in my legs, but I pushed through and stood using the tree for support. Kyro walked toward me emitting lightning from his body while raising his right arm in my direction.

"Even if you are from the Hikari Tribe, you're in no condition to block me." Kyro said as he sent a bolt of lightning right at me.

Before I could respond, the lightning was within just a few inches from my face, but it didn't touch me somehow. The lightning went flying to the right of me as if it was being pulled.

Then, the lightning hit a really tall bizarre looking tree. It looked like a big rod with spiked branches and no leaves. At the top of the tree was Lucius, standing on its flat surface.

"Salutations!" He shouted while waving.

I couldn't help but smile as I saw that lightning from other locations in the city all being pulled to the tree. Kyro eyes widened as he saw Lucius and began to totally freak out.

He shouted, "NO!" Then he just started screaming while shaking his head back and forth. The scream was intense and echoed throughout the tribe.

Lucius and I were both stunned by Kyro's outburst. Then, suddenly, three giant Crimson Bloods came running toward me from behind.

Lucius shouted, "Don't worry, Bro! I'm on it."

Lucius held his hands together as if he was praying. Then, a blast of pure white lightning came from the big rod-like tree. The lightning took out two of the three Crimsons at the same time. One of them was able to avoid the attack and continued running in my direction.

Lucius shouted, "I'm out of ammo!"

Before I could do anything, the giant ran and jumped right over me as if I wasn't even there. That's when I noticed that it was the Bull-like hybrid that I fought before. The hybrid picked up Kyro and put him on his back.

Kyro said, "Mote, you are my most reliable."

Kyro bit into Mote's shoulder. The giant hybrid screamed as if he was in pain, yet he allowed Kyro to continue to bite him. Kyro appeared to be sucking the blood from the giant crimson. At that moment, I noticed that Mote appeared to be shrinking.

Before long, he was almost back to normal size, except he looked older and extremely malnourished. Then, I noticed that Kyro's entire body was beginning to heal. Even his left arm seemed to be growing back, and two black horns began to emerge from Kyro's head. It wasn't long before every injury that I'd inflicted on him was healed.

Kyro began laughing, "I feel great! I knew it! HA! I knew it! But I'd never dream that it would have such an effect on me. My arm is even growing back! It won't be long before it's back to normal."

"What just happened?" I asked.

Kyro responded, "I just consumed my own formula that was flowing through his blood. I thought that it might make me physically larger , but it worked more internally and healed my wounds by multiplying and amplifying my cells. Which is extremely effective for me since it contains my own blood. This explains why these beautiful horns are now growing from my head. I always wanted horns! You can't imagine the envy I felt when I gave these losers my blood, and the got horns when I've never had them. But, there they are now. Ha, ha, ha! Just in case you can't tell, I'm much stronger than I was before. When you fought me I was already injured. Now, I'm at one hundred percent!"

I shouted, "I don't need to be at one hundred percent to take you down!"

Kyro shouted, "Such a bold statement from such a tiny speck! But, just to be sure…"

Kyro jumped backwards about 200 feet.

"…I'm going to beat you from a distance. Then, I'll take out the rest of this Umi Tribe trash, not to mention our Shido friend up there."

Kyro took a deep breath and smiled. Then, he blew out a massive cloud of brownish-green toxic smoke. I was trapped. Lucius was too far away to help me, and I was too injured to run. I tried to run, but the toxic smoke was moving too fast. It was obvious that I wasn't going to make it. Suddenly, I heard a female voice shout, "Shōkan!"

Chapter Twenty Three
Yumi

All of the smoke was pushed upward and back toward Kyro. I turned around, expecting to see Princess Tuyette standing behind me, but I saw Juicy gliding downward like she was riding the wind.

When she landed she said, "Yo! What up? You good?"

"Thanks to you, I am. How did you do that?"

"Not important! We don't have much time before the smoke clears. I have to get you all to safety…but where to go, where to go?"

I looked around. Then, I looked to the top of the tree that Lucius was standing on, but Lucius was gone.

I said, "Where did he go?"

Juicy responded, "Who?"

"Lucius, he was up there. He just saved me not long ago."

"Where was he?" she asked.

"Up there." I said as I pointed with my left hand to the top of the rod-like tree.

"That's perfect!" Juicy said as she ran toward the princess.

The princess smiled, "Hey Juicy! I see you're back from your assignment. How did it go?"

"It was going fine until I heard that our tribe was being attacked. So, I put the assignment on hold. By the way, I prefer to be called my real name now."

Oh, okay, Yumi." The princess said as she thought to herself, 'She's finally decided to get serious.'

Juicy put the Princess on one shoulder and Dan on the other and summoned ocean water under her feet. They surfed to the base of the tree where long, sharp rods stuck out the most, which protected them from flying debris and direct attacks.

Juicy checked Dan's pulse, "He's alive but barely. He needs medical attention as soon as possible."

As Juicy came back, the toxic smoke was nearly cleared.

"Juicy lend me your sword." I asked.

"Yeah, right? You can barely stand, and you think I'm going to give you MY sword? You're better off over there with the them."

As the smoke cleared, Juicy began walking forward. As she saw who we had been fighting, she put her hand on her hip and said, "Well if it isn't Dr. Kyro! I should have known that you were a hybrid, considering how bad your breath is."

"Well, if it isn't the vulgar, loud-mouth and lazy successor of Princess Tuyette."

"That's right! And this vulgar, loud-mouth is about to put you in your place!"

Kyro snarled with anger, ran toward Juicy and blew a massive stream of fire at her. Juicy stood there and didn't even bother dodging his attack. The fire appeared to hit Juicy. It looked as if she was entirely consumed by it, but the fire soon cleared as she spat out a massive amount of water from her mouth. This created a massive cloud of steam in the air.

The steam cleared revealing that neither Juicy nor Kyro was injured by their scuffle.

Just a moment later, as Kyro was about to charge again, there was a beeping sound just like before.

The princess' eyes widened, "Oh no, not again. We have to

get out of here!"

Kyro pulled out his pocket watch and smiled, "You may be able to block my fire, but you can't block what's coming."

"What do you mean?" Juicy said hastily.

Kyro began to laugh, "They're getting bigger as we speak! But this time, they're not just going to attack! THEY ARE GOING TO EXPLODE!"
"What are you talking about?" Juicy yelled.

The princess shouted with great desperation in her voice, "The Crimsons! The last time that thing beeped they became giants!"

"I see. So, now they are about to get even bigger and then explode." Juicy said as she glared at Kyro.

Kyro laughed, "Each one of them will completely destroy everything within a thirty yard radius!"

Then, I spoke up, "Well, what about you? You just drank the formula! How do you plan on escaping?"

"Don't be concerned about me! I am a true Crimson Blood! I won't be exploding! You best worry about yourselves because the others will explode very soon!" Kyro claimed.

I became irritated, "So, you're sacrificing all of your followers?"

"Sacrifice? They volunteered!" Kyro shouted.

I tried to step forward to attack Kyro but my body was still too injured and I fell to one knee.

Juicy said, "Don't let him get you worked up. Besides, I'll take him from here on out."

Then we heard a very low deep voice say, "That will not be necessary."

We all looked around but did not see anyone.

Kyro looked above him and said, "They should have been getting bigger by now. What happened to the explosions?"

Then, Lucius showed up, slowly approaching us from behind, "I happened to them, well, most of them. These guys happened to the rest of them." Then he pointed behind Kyro.

Behind Kyro were three hybrids wearing chest armor with a dragon foot symbol slightly different from Kyro's Crimson Blood symbol.

One of the hybrids looked like a Gorilla, his arms and shoulders were massive. The other looked like a snake, the bottom half of his body was just one long tail--he had no legs and appeared to slither around on his belly. The last hybrid looked like a lion, and it was obvious that he was the one in charge.

Lucius continued, "When I saw Dr. Kyro drink that hybrid's blood, and it began to shrink I knew exactly what to do to take out the rest of the hybrids. So, I summoned my cleansing mushroom plant and attached a seed to each giant Crimson. The mushrooms sucked all of the contents of Dr. Kyro's serum out."

"That means..." Kyro snarled.

Lucius continued, "Which means that they're looking human again, well mostly. But those guys over there, they killed the Crimsons that I couldn't get to. Although I'm grateful...I must say, I'm a little confused seeing that they appear to be Crimsons too."

All of a sudden we heard that same low deep voice again, but this time it was closer to us.

It said, "Let me explain." Then from behind us near the princess came the lion-like hybrid that was not long before behind Kyro.

 I wondered, 'How did he? When did he? Who the heck are these guys?'

Chapter Twenty Four

Crimson Bloods

He spoke softly and clearly, "We are the true Crimson Bloods. We have come to clear our name. You MUST know that we, the true Crimson Bloods, have not been stealing from you. Until now, we have not been trespassing into your territories. Most importantly, we have not been killing the Shido Tribe citizens. We, the true Crimson Bloods, established our own peaceful society long ago. In fact, the one you know as Dr. Kyro is one of our own. Therefore, we will punish him ourselves for his indiscretions."

"What are you talking about? I've been alone from the beginning. I've never even heard of any other Crimsons! If I had known of such a place…" Kyro shouted then paused as he bit his lip.

The lion-like Crimson continued, "The only thing that would explain why you never returned would be that you somehow lost your memory."

The princess slowly stood using the branches from the lightning rod tree, "Where is your civilization?"

"Princess, with all due respect, that is none of your concern. Although I am here to help you today, understand that tomorrow is a new day, and we have not forgotten that it was your father who nearly wiped out our kind."

Then Juicy shouted, "So, you expect us to say thank you and let you go! How do we know that you aren't the masterminds behind this whole thing?"

"Understand, we, the true Crimson Bloods did not want our existence to even be discovered. We wanted to remain a secret society. But, when we heard news that the Crimsons have returned and have been making trouble, we, the true Crimson Bloods, were forced to investigate. And we were willing to reveal our existence prematurely in order to clear our name."

The princess shouted, "He worked for me and I didn't even know what he was doing! How did you find out?"

The lion-like Crimson said, "If you seek, you will find."

Tuyette was speechless. We all were. The veterans who helped fight off the fake Crimsons all began to surround the area, staring at the true Crimson Bloods.

Suddenly, we all heard running footsteps grow louder and louder. Then we heard a very robot-like voice say, "Doctor, Doctor, I'm here."

It was Jack Findle still in his hospital clothes, with his butt hanging out of his gown, and a metal device around his neck.

He continued to speak in his robotic voice, "Don't worry Doctor. Your plan will still work. Just as I always thought; I am your greatest asset."

Lucius shouted, "Don't laugh guys, that's all he wants you to do. Talking bout asset."

Everyone but Kyro and Lucius began laughing. Even the true Crimson Bloods cracked a smile.

Jack said, "You won't be laughing soon because you'll all be dead. I took a double dose of your explosive serum doctor. Aren't you proud of me? We are finally going to rid ourselves of this Umi trash."

Kyro smiled, "Jack, my boy. You finally did something right!"

Then Kyro turned in attempt to run away, but the gorilla-like Crimson quickly took him down. He hammered Kyro in the head and hit him so hard that half of his body was cratered into the ground. The only part of Kyro we could see was his legs.

Jack tried to shout with his robotic-like voice but every

word was monotone. He said, "Dr. Kyro, nooooooo. I will avenge you."

Then, Jack's body began to rapidly swell. Jack attempted to shout in his robot voice again, "Look who's laughing now. Ha, ha, ha."

Suddenly, we all began to feel the heat from Jack's body rise as his body began to glow.

Juicy shouted, "Run!"

But it was too late for us all, Princess Tuyette, Dan Siratchi, Juicy, Lucius, all of the Umi Tribe veterans, Myself and even the true Crimson Bloods.

The explosions wiped out everything in a sixty yard radius.

Chapter Twenty Five

Chief Dawn

In a blink of an eye, everyone was gliding off of the ground miles away from the explosion towards the shorelines. It was almost like the impact of the explosion blew us back-ward. But for some reason we all we gliding in the same direction.

We all landed safely on the beach at the edge of the Umi Tribe. As we all stood up and tried to figure out what hap-pened we saw a tall, dark man, wearing a large Hikari Tribe medallion.

He turned to us with a concerned look on his face and said, "Is everyone alright?"

Lucius said, "That was scary."

Some of the veterans were clinching their hearts and Master Kim Lee said, "Does anyone have any spare adult diapers?"

Before anyone could ask who he was, we all were distracted by an army of men coming out of the ocean. As they walked forward, the water parted. It was the Umi Tribe Protectors. Within the crowd of protectors there were people that I recognized like Brodie and Steve, but there were also people that I've never seen before. Leading the army was the Umi Tribe Chief, Dawn Umi.

Chief Dawn walked over to the man who saved us, "What in the world is going on?"

"Not much, now. It appears to be over."

"What happened?"

"I'm not exactly sure. I actually just got here. Maybe you should ask your daughter over there."

The man said as he pointed to Juicy.

"She's not my daughter. She's my niece. My daughter is over there," Chief Dawn said as he pointed at Princess Tuyette.

The man said, "Wow, That's Tooty?"

Chief Dawn turned to him, "Watch it!"

The man began laughing, "Just as uptight as ever, huh?"

Chief Dawn walked over to Tuyette, "What happened here?"

Tuyette, still injured, said, "I'll tell you on the way to the infirmary. Many of us need immediate medical attention. Please have your men take us there." She said as she looked at Dan Siratchi.

Chief Dawn said, "Very well. The infirmary appears to still be standing."

As Chief Dawn picked her up, Tuyette began talking with tears in her eyes, "You know how history repeats itself, well that Great War from fifteen years ago just happened all over again."

On our way to the infirmary, some of us were being carried while others walked. There were a lot of people who had injuries, even the man who saved us was limping for some reason.

The Princess began telling Chief Dawn everything that happened. She explained how Kyro was secretly a Crimson Blood and how he manipulated his way into the Umi Tribe as a scientist. She explained Dr. Kyro's relationship with Dr. Cyrus and how Kyro was even responsible for the previous war. She explained everything up to the moment that we landed on the beach.

Chief Dawn's facial expression didn't change once the entire time she was talking. When she finally got to the end of her story, we were all together in a large hospital room that seated multiple patients.

She said, "Then, Jack Findle exploded and we all would be dead now if it had not been for the Chief Kazan there. I assume he used that legendary teleportation technique of his to save us. We will forever be grateful and in his debt."

Chief Kazan nodded and smiled.

I was amazed! At that moment, I realized that I was in the presence of two Shōkan Chiefs! That's when I thought about what that old lady named Winter professed to me earlier, 'I see royalty in your future… also see destruction…', I was in awe.

Chief Dawn said, "So that's what happened, huh? It seems to me that Dr. Kyro wanted you to call me and my troops here so that he could take us all down in those final blasts. You made a good decision, Tuyette."

Chief Dawn turned to the princess, "Your story also explains why your men used my technique to transport themselves to our underwater city. When they arrived, they had their suspicions about there being an attack on the Tribe but none of them were sure."

Chief Kazan stepped in, "By the way, how is that possible? The Hikari Tribe is the only tribe known to have teleportation techniques. How could your men teleport from a collapsing building into an underwater city?"

"My technique is not a teleportation technique like yours.

It is more like a summoning technique. We Umi Tribe shōkans can summon water from any spot in the ocean. Just as you can summon heat, light, and radiation from any spot of the sun. When the transaction of summoning occurs, a microscopic portal is under our control. I've learned to expand that portal and reverse the summoning. Of course, it's rare for one to master such a technique, that's why I had Master Kim Lee to teach them how to execute this technique as a team, just in case something like this were to happen, and it was a good thing that I did."

"So, instead of summoning water to your current location, you summon yourself to the location from where you normally summon water from. Which would mean that it's a one way trip and that you couldn't transport yourself back to where you came from."

"You make it sound more complicated than it is, but yes, that's right."

"Okay, so that's why it took you guys so long to get back here." Chief Kazan said while smiling.

Lucius walked forward and bowed, "Greetings, Great Shōkan Leaders. I am the future Shido Tribe Chief. In fact, it was actually just made official yesterday. May I intervene? I have a question for Princess Tuyette."

Chief Dawn said, "Go ahead."

Lucius nodded, "Your Highness, why didn't you listen to Corvi's warning?"

The princess looked puzzled, "She never warned me about anything!"

Lucius looked puzzled.

"No, she never told me anything. Did she know about Kyro?"

Lucius froze in silence and began to stare off in space then turned to Tuyette, smiled and said, "No, of course not. I meant about the possibility of an attack."

"Well, if that's what you meant, then, yes, we talked about that often?"

"Okay thanks. Well, I have to be leaving now." Lucius insisted.

Chief Dawn said, "Wait and rest here. Then, leave in the morning. I would like to honor you for what you've done for our Tribe."

Lucius smiled, "I didn't do it to be honored, Sir: I did it because it was my duty as a fellow shōkan. So, thanks, but no thanks. Although, I really appreciate the gesture."

Chief Dawn nodded, "Then, safe travels to you, future Chief

of Shido. By the way, how is your father?"

Lucius smiled as he was leaving and said, "He's still as jolly as ever."

As Lucius walked out, Kazan suddenly shouted, "Oh my gosh! I totally forgot about Herona! She's waiting on me to report back! I left her in Mums Village to check things out here. I told her that I would be right back, but when I got here I ended up having to help out because of that explosion. I'll be right back, You Guys! By the way, Chief Dawn, I just thought about this while they were talking, but you might want to invest in underwater radio transmissions. See you guys in a few."

Before Chief Dawn could respond in anger, I interrupted.

"WAIT!" I shouted. "Were you talking about my mother, Herona? Herona Kumoi-Siratchi?"

Chief Kazan said, "Yes, that's her!"

I sat up in my hospital bed, "How do you know her?"

"I'll tell you when I get back," he said as his entire body began to glow. Even his skin and eyes illuminated. There was a big flash of light, and he vanished. As he left there was a powerful wind that blew. Then, I noticed Dan, who was still unconscious.

Moments later, Kazan returned with my mother. They walked into the room through the door casually as if he didn't even teleport earlier. When my mother saw me, tears of joy and relief swelled up in her eyes. She walked to my bed and hugged me as she wept.

She looked at me and said, "I was so worried about you. I'm so glad that you're okay."

Then, she signaled for Chief Kazan to come. Kazan limped over to us.

She said, "Kazai, I would like to introduce you to your birth father, Chief Kazan of the Hikari Tribe."

My dad said, "I know I don't know you very well yet but I am already very proud of you!"

"Thanks," I said as tears welled up in my eyes.

It felt like all of my problems and pain melted away just for that moment. We all hugged as tears streamed from all of our eyes.

I looked at my mother, "Mom."

"What is it?" She responded.

"Just so you know, bringing my Dad here makes up for everything that I've been through. Thank you"

She smiled and hugged me even tighter and said, "Is that your way of saying that you forgive me?"

I just smiled and hugged her tighter.

Chapter Twenty Six

Conclusion

The next day, Chief Dawn publicly honored everyone who played a major role in protecting the Umi Tribe. The ceremony was held outside of the infirmary, one of the only places in the tribe that didn't need repairs.

The ceremony broadcasted on radio and video transmissions. Although he was still in a coma, Dan Siratchi was honored. He was given the Hero's Badge of Honor. My mom accepted it in his absence.

Princess Tuyette, who was in a wheelchair, was honored with a new medallion for her bravery and wisdom.

Master Kim Lee was honored with early retirement and a golden plaque. Lucius and Chief Kazan were named as honorary members of the Umi Tribe for the roles that they played in saving the lives of our tribe's citizens.

I was honored as well. I was given a brand new sword made from platinum.

Juicy (aka Yumi) received the highest honor of us all. She was given what they called a Shōkan Blade. It seemed to be really important, but all I knew was that it was an old relic from our shōkan ancestors.

Basically, everyone was honored except for the ones that actually defeated Kyro--the true Crimson Bloods. We never found their remains or even the remains of Kyro. We all assumed that they got caught in the blast, but to be honest we didn't really know. The counterfeit crimsons that survived were taken to the underwater city to be imprisoned. Knowing Chief Dawn, they all will eventually be executed.

The next day, the princess told me that I was never officially an Umi Tribe protector because I named Dan Siratchi as my father instead of Chief Kazan. So, she gave me a choice: I could start the process to become an Umi Tribe Protector all over again, or I could go back to the Hikari Tribe with my father.

Although I decided to go to the Hikari Tribe with Chief Kazan, my doctor said that I couldn't leave until my body was back to normal, especially my legs, which could take a while. Either way, I decided that I wouldn't leave until Dan Siratchi had awakened from his coma so that I could say my goodbyes and thank him for getting me as far as I am.

It turned out that my injuries and the princess' were very similar. After talking for a while, we all, including the doctors, determined that our injuries were the result of us trying to use unperfected modes: Wind and Light. This conversation led to Chief Kazan finding out that the Hikari Dragon trained me. He immediately left to visit Gomorra City.

When he arrived, he found that the city's sign had fallen down, and the Hikari Dragon's name was removed from the sign. After asking around, Kazan still didn't get any information on where he could find the Hikari Dragon. All he knew for sure was that he was no longer in the city.

Being stuck in the infirmary was a drag, but it wasn't so bad with friends stopping by. Juicy came by almost everyday, sometimes she would bring Broadie with her. Lucius visited once but he didn't stay long and seemed to be in a hurry. My mother bounced from my room to Dan's room about every ten minutes.

Almost everyday that went by the princess would ask her doctor a certain question and everyday she would get the same answer until one day when the princess asked: "Is my father still here?"

Her doctor said, "No, Chief Dawn has returned back to Reef City."

The princess sat up and said, "Contact Hugo immediately!"

Her doctor said, "You mean, The Hurricane? But hasn't he been exiled by your father himself?"

The princess said, "I am aware of that. But as long as my father isn't here, I'm in charge! And you and I both know that Hugo is the only one who can heal me, so you get him here and you do it NOW!"

Introduction to book two

The Heartfruit

Ever since Lucius found out that Corvi didn't tell Tuyette about Kyro, he became suspicious of her. As a result of his espionage, he discovered that Corvi has a secret lab that she called her garden. In this garden, he found that there were caged animoids and many bizarre plants and experimentations. Out of all of the bizarre plants, there was one plant in particular that stood out from the rest: the branches looked similar to human arms; the bark was like callused skin; the leaves were like human hair; and the fruit were heart-shaped and even appeared to have veins.

Corvi had a picture of Kyro in her hands. She placed it at the base of the massive tree. "What a fool he was. I knew that he would fail. If I hadn't covered his trail so many times he definitely would not have gotten as far as he did. Shucks, without my research or the fruit from this tree, he would have never been able to make those people into hybrids in the first place." Corvi smiled, "Although his plan failing was part of my plan, I never imagined that it would uncover the existence of the actual Crimson Bloods. That works out even better for me. With their fear of the Crimsons, all of the tribes will be like putty in my hands. All those lives that I had to take will not be in vain. Isn't that right, Lucius?" Corvi turned to Lucius who was hiding behind one of Corvi's trees.

Lucius couldn't move. He was frozen in fear.

www.ingramcontent.com/pod-product-compliance
Lightning Source LLC
Chambersburg PA
CBHW021424110726
47901CB00008B/2284